To: Patrick Knight
<patrick.knight@mymail.com>

From: Molly Cooper
<molly.cooper@flowermail.com>

Subject: Impossible dreams

I assume from your silence that you're not going to pass on any wise advice about how I might find my dream Englishman.

Patrick, have you any idea how hard it is?

I don't mean it's hard to get myself asked out. My question is—would you believe how hard it is to find the right *style* of man?

Some people would say my dream of dating an English gentleman is completely unrealistic. Mind you, my definition of *gentleman* is elastic. I'm mainly talking about his manners and his clothes and, well yes, his voice. I do adore a posh English accent.

I know it's a lot to ask. I mean, if such a man existed why would he be interested in a very ordinary Australian girl? Apparently, on a given night out in London there is a 0.0000034 percent chance of meeting the right person.

That's a 1 in 285,000 chance.

You'd have better odds if you went to the cane toad races, Patrick. Of winning some money, I mean, not finding the perfect date.

But then you're not looking for romance. Are you?

Molly

Do you like stories that are fun and flirty?

Then you'll ♥ Harlequin® Romance's new miniseries—
where love and laughter are guaranteed!

If you love romantic comedies, look for

The Fun Factor

Warm and witty stories of falling in love

**Look out for the next
in the Fun Factor series...coming soon.**

BARBARA HANNAY

Molly Cooper's Dream Date

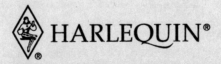

TORONTO • NEW YORK • LONDON
AMSTERDAM • PARIS • SYDNEY • HAMBURG
STOCKHOLM • ATHENS • TOKYO • MILAN • MADRID
PRAGUE • WARSAW • BUDAPEST • AUCKLAND

Recycling programs
for this product may
not exist in your area.

ISBN-13: 978-0-373-74077-2

MOLLY COOPER'S DREAM DATE

First North American Publication 2011

Barbara Hannay was born in Sydney, educated in Brisbane and has spent most of her adult life living in tropical North Queensland, where she and her husband have raised four children. While she has enjoyed many happy times camping and canoeing in the bush, she also delights in an urban lifestyle—chamber music, contemporary dance, movies and dining out. An English teacher, she has always loved writing, and now, by having her stories published, she is living her most cherished fantasy. Visit her website at www.barbarahannay.com.

Special thanks to Jenny Haddon whose
wonderful London hospitality inspired this story.

CHAPTER ONE

'THIS is my favourite part,' Molly whispered as the glamorous couple on her TV screen walked sadly but stoically to opposite ends of London's Westminster Bridge. 'He's going to turn back to her any minute now.'

Molly was curled on her couch in a tense ball. Karli, at the other end of the couch, helped herself to more popcorn.

'Don't miss this, Karli. I cry every time. Look. He hears Big Ben, and he stops, and—' Molly's voice broke on a sob. 'He turns.' She hugged her knees. 'See the look on his face?'

'Ohhh…' Karli let out a hushed breath. 'You can see he really, *really* loves her.'

'I know. It's so beautiful.' Molly reached for tissues as the gorgeous hero stood alone on the bridge, stricken-faced, shoulders squared, waiting for the woman in the long fur coat to turn back to him.

Karli grabbed a cushion and clutched it to her chest. 'He'll chase after her.'

'No. It's up to her now. If she doesn't turn back, he knows she doesn't love him.'

On the screen, a red double-decker London bus slowed to a stop and the movie's heroine, in her ankle-length, glamorous coat, hurried to catch it.

'No,' Karli moaned as the bus took off with the woman on board, and the camera switched to another close-up of the hero's grimly devastated face. 'Don't tell me it's a sad ending.'

Molly pressed her lips together to stop herself from speaking. The camera tracked upwards to a bird's eye view of London, showing the silvery River Thames curving below, and the Houses of Parliament, Big Ben...the solitary figure of the hero standing on Westminster Bridge...and the red bus driving away.

Karli was scowling. Molly hugged her knees tighter, gratified that her friend was hooked into the tension.

The camera climbed higher still, and the London bus was matchbox-size. The sounds of the city traffic were replaced by music—violins swelling with lush and aching beauty.

Molly had seen this movie more than a dozen times, but tears still rolled down her cheeks.

And then...at last...

At *last*…

The bus stopped.

The tiny figure of the heroine emerged…

The camera swooped down once more, zooming closer and closer as the lovers ran towards each other, arms outstretched, embracing at last.

The credits began to roll. Karli wrinkled her nose. 'OK. I admit that wasn't bad.'

'Not bad?' Molly sniffed. 'I suppose that's why you practically bit a piece out of my sofa cushion? Come on—admit it's amazing. The look on Christian's face when he thinks he's lost Vanessa is *the* most emotional moment in cinematic history.' She gave a dramatic sigh. 'And London has to be the most romantic city in the world.'

Shrugging, Karli reached for more popcorn. 'Isn't Paris supposed to be the most romantic city?'

'No way. Not for me. Paris is—Paris is… Oh, I don't know.' Molly gave a helpless flap of her hands. 'Paris just…isn't London.'

'Admit it, Mozza. You have a thing for English guys. You're convinced that London is full of perfect gentlemen.'

It was best to ignore her friend's sarcasm. Molly wasn't going to admit that it held a grain—OK, maybe even more than a grain—of truth. Her love affair with London was deeply personal.

Pressing the remote to turn the set off, she went to the window and looked out into the night. The moon was almost full and it silvered the tall pines on the headland and the smooth, sparkling surface of the Coral Sea.

'One thing's for sure,' she said. 'Nothing romantic like that is ever going to happen to me. Not on this island.'

'Oh, I don't know. Our island might not have Big Ben or Westminster Bridge, but the moonlight on Picnic Bay's not bad. I wasn't complaining when Jimbo proposed.'

Molly smiled as she turned from the window. 'Sorry. I wasn't counting you and Jimbo. You guys are as romantic as it gets—best friends since kindergarten. Everyone here knew you'd end up together.'

'Well, to be honest, it's not exactly romantic when your husband spends half his life away on a fishing trawler.'

'I guess.' Molly moved to the kitchen and reached for a saucepan to make hot chocolate. 'I shouldn't keep watching that movie. It always makes me restless—makes me want to take off and live in London.'

'Does it have to be London? If you want to get off the island, why don't you try Sydney or Brisbane? Even Cairns?'

Molly rolled her eyes. As if any Australian city could live up to her vision of England's famous capital. For as long as she could remember, she'd been entranced by London—by its history, its buildings, its pageantry, its culture.

She loved all the names—like Portobello Road, the Serpentine, Piccadilly Circus and Battersea. For her they had a thrilling, magical ring. Like poetry.

Karli shrugged. 'If I went overseas, I'd rather go to America. Jimbo's going to take me to Las Vegas.'

'Wow. When?'

'One day. *Ha-ha*. If either of us ever gets a job with better pay.'

'Money's my problem, too. The mortgage on this place uses up most of my savings. And the rent in London's horrendous. I've checked on the internet.'

'But you might be able to manage it if you rented out this place.'

Molly shuddered. Renting this cottage would mean a series of strangers living here, and it wouldn't seem right when it had been her gran's home for more than fifty years.

'Or,' said Karli, 'what about a house swap? That way you'd get to pick who lives here, and it would only be for a short time. My cousin in

Cairns swapped with a couple from Denmark, and it worked out fine.'

'A house swap?' A tingling sensation danced down Molly's spine. 'How does that work?'

Patrick Knight glared at the towering pile of paperwork on his desk, and then he glared at his watch. Past eight already, and he would be here for hours yet.

Grimacing, he picked up his mobile phone and thumbed a hasty text message. Angela was *not* going to like this, but it couldn't be helped.

Ange, so sorry. Snowed under at work. Will have to bow out of tonight. Can we make a date for Friday instead? P

Snapping the phone closed, Patrick reached for the next folder in the pile. His stomach growled, and along with his hunger pangs he felt a surge of frustration.

The past years of global financial crisis had seen his job in London's banking world morph from an interesting and challenging career into a source of constant stress.

It was like working in a war zone. Too many of his colleagues had been fired, or had resigned.

Some had even suffered nervous breakdowns. At times he'd felt like the last man standing.

Yes, it was true that he *had* saved a couple of major accounts, but he was doing the work of three people in his department, and the shower of commendations from his boss had rather lost their shine. He'd reached the point where he had to ask why he was slogging away, working ridiculous hours and giving everything he had to his job, when his life outside the office was—

Non-existent.

Truth was, he no longer *had* a life away from the bank. No time to enjoy the lovely house he'd bought in Chelsea, no time to go out with his latest girlfriend. How he'd managed to meet Angela in the first place was a miracle, but almost certainly she would give up on him soon—just as her predecessors had.

As for the crazy, *crazy* promise he'd once made to himself that he would balance his working life with writing a novel. In his spare time. Ha-ha.

Except for Patrick it was no longer a laughing matter. This was *his* life, or rather his *non*-life, and he was wasting it. One day he'd wake up and discover he was fifty—like his boss—pale, anxious, boring and only able to talk about one thing. Work.

His mobile phone pinged. It was Angela, as expected. Tight-jawed, he clicked on her reply.

Sorry. Not Friday. Not ever. One cancellation too many. Goodbye, sweet P. Ange

Patrick cursed, but he couldn't really blame Ange. Tomorrow he'd send her two—no, three dozen roses. But he suspected they wouldn't do the trick. Not this time. If he was honest, he couldn't pretend that her rejection would break his heart— but it *was* symptomatic of the depths to which his life had sunk.

In a burst of anger, he pushed his chair back from his desk and began to prowl.

The office felt like a prison. It *was* a damn prison, and he felt a mad urge to break out of it.

Actually, it wasn't a mad urge. It was a highly reasonable and justified need. A must.

In mid-prowl, his eyes fell on the globe of the world that he'd salvaged from the old boardroom when it had been refurbished—in those giddy days before the financial world had gone belly up. Now it sat in the corner of his office, and lately he'd stared at it often, seized by a longing to be any-where on that tiny sphere.

Anywhere except London.

Walking towards it now, Patrick spun the globe and watched the coloured shapes of the continents swirl. He touched it with his finger, feeling the friction as its pace slowed.

If I were free, I'd go anywhere. When this globe stops spinning, I'll go wherever my finger is pointing.

The globe stopped. Patrick laughed. He'd been thinking of somewhere exotic, like Tahiti or Rio de Janeiro, but his finger was resting on the east coast of Australia. A tiny dot. An island.

He leaned closer to read the fine print. Magnetic Island.

Never heard of it.

About to dismiss it, he paused. *I said I'd go anywhere—anywhere in the world. Why don't I at least look this place up?*

But why bother? It wasn't as if it could happen. He wouldn't be going anywhere. He was locked in here.

But what if I made it happen? Surely it's time?

Back at his desk, Patrick tried a quick internet search for Magnetic Island, and his eyebrows lifted as the first page of links scrolled down. The island was clearly a tourist destination, with palm trees and white sand and blue tropical seas. Not so different from Tahiti, perhaps?

The usual variety of accommodations was offered. Then two words leapt out at him from the bottom of the screen: *House Swap.*

Intrigued, Patrick hit the link.

House Swap: Magnetic Island, Queensland, Australia

2 bedroom cottage

Location Details: Nestled among trees on a headland, this home has ocean views and is only a three-minute walk through the national park to a string of beautiful bays. Close to the Great Barrier Reef, the island provides a water wonderland for sailing, canoeing, parasailing, fishing and diving.

Preferred Swap Dates: From 1st April—flexible

Preferred Swap Length: Three to four months

Preferred Destination: London, UK

Patrick grinned. For a heady moment he could picture himself there—in a different hemisphere, in a different world.

Free, free...

Swimming with coral fishes. Lying in a hammock beneath palm trees. Checking out bikini-clad Australian girls. Writing the fabulous thriller that resided only in his head. Typing it on his laptop while looking out at the sparkling blue sea.

OK, amusement over. Nose back to the grindstone.

With great reluctance, he lifted a folder of computer printouts from the pile and flipped it open.

But his concentration was shot to pieces. His mind couldn't settle on spreadsheets and figures. He was composing a description of his house for a similar swapping advertisement.

Home Exchange: Desirable Chelsea, London, UK
3 bedroom house with garden
Close to public transport and amenities—two-minute walk.
* Television
* Fireplaces
* Balcony/patio
* Dining/shopping nearby
* Galleries/museums
Available for three-month exchange: April/May to June/July
Destination—Coastal Queensland, Australia

Two and a half hours later Patrick had closed the last folder, and he'd also reached a decision.

He would do it. He had to. He would get away. He would make an appointment with his boss. First thing in the morning.

CHAPTER TWO

To: Patrick Knight <patrick.knight@mymail.com>
From: Molly Cooper <molly.cooper@flower-mail.com>
Subject: We're off—like a rotten egg

Hi Patrick

I can't believe I'll actually be in England in just over twenty-four hours. At last I'm packed (suitcases groaning), and my little house is shining clean and ready for you. Brand-new sheets on the bed—I hope you like navy blue.

I also hope you'll feel welcome here and, more importantly, comfortable. I considered leaving flowers in a vase, but I was worried they might droop and die and start to smell before you got here. I'll leave the key under the flowerpot beside the back door.

Now, I know that probably sounds incredibly reckless to you, but don't worry—the residents of Magnetic Island are very honest and extremely laid-back. No one locks their doors.

I don't want you to fret, though, so I've also left a spare key at Reception at the Sapphire Bay resort, where I used to work until yesterday.

Used to work.

That has such a nice ring, doesn't it? I've trained Jill, the owner's niece, to take my place while I'm away, and for now, at least, I'm giddily carefree and unemployed.

Yippee!!

You have no idea how much I've always wanted to live in London, even if it's only for three months. Thanks to you, Patrick, this really is my dream come true, and I'm beyond excited. I don't think I'll be able to sleep tonight.

Have you finished up at your work? Are you having a farewell party? Mine was last night. It was pretty rowdy, and I have no idea what to do with all the gifts people gave me. I can't fit as much as another peanut in my suitcases, so I'll probably have to stash these things in a box under my bed (your bed now). Sorry.

By the way, please feel free to use my car. It's not much more than a sardine can on wheels, but it gets you about. Don't worry that it's unregistered. Cars on the island don't need registration unless they're taken over to the mainland.

It was kind of you to mention that your car is garaged just around the corner from your place, but don't worry, I won't risk my shaky driving skills in London traffic.

Oh, and don't be upset if the ferry is running late. The boats here run on 'island time'.

Anyway, happy travels.

London, here I come!

Molly

PS I agree that we shouldn't phone each other except in the direst emergency. You're right—phone calls can be intrusive (especially with a ten-hour time difference). And they're costly. E-mails are so handy—and I'll try to be diplomatic. No guarantees. I can rattle on when I'm excited.

M

To: Molly Cooper <molly.cooper@flowermail. com>
From: Patrick Knight <patrick.knight@mymail. com>
Subject: Re: We're off—like a rotten egg
Dear Molly

Thanks for your message. No time for a fare-well party, I'm afraid. Had to work late to get my desk cleared. Rushing now to pack and get away. Cidalia (cleaning lady) will come in some time this week to explain everything about the house—how the oven works, etc.

The keys to the house are in a safety deposit box at the Chelsea branch of the bank I work for on the King's Road. It's a square brick building. My colleagues have instructions to hand the keys over to you—and I've left a map. You'll just need to show your passport. You shouldn't have any problems.

Have a good flight.

Best wishes

Patrick

To: Patrick Knight <patrick.knight@mymail.com>
From: Molly Cooper <molly.cooper@flower-mail.com>
Subject: I'm in London!!!!!!!

Wow! Wow! Wow! Wow! Wow! Wow! Wow! Wow!

If I wasn't so tired I'd pinch myself, but I'm horribly jet-lagged and can hardly keep my eyes open. Insanely happy, though.

Your very gentlemanly colleague at the bank

handed over the keys and wished me a pleasant stay at number thirty-four Alice Grove, and
then I trundled my luggage around the corner
and—

Patrick, your house is—
Indescribably
Lovely.

Divine will have to suffice for now, but the
truth is that your home is more than divine.

Too tired to do it justice tonight. Will have
my first English cup of tea and fall into bed.
Your bed. Gosh, that sounds rather intimate,
doesn't it? Will write tomorrow.

Blissfully
Molly

To: Patrick Knight <patrick.knight@mymail.
com>
From: Molly Cooper <molly.cooper@flower-
mail.com>
Subject: Thank you

Hi Patrick

I've slept for ten hours in your lovely king-
size bed and am feeling much better today,
but my head is still buzzing with excitement!
I've never left Australia before, so my first sight
of England yesterday was the most amazing
thrill. We flew in over the English Channel, and

when I saw the green and misty fields, just the way I've always imagined them, I confess I became a tad weepy.

And then Heathrow. Oh, my God, what an experience. Now I know how cattle feel when they're being herded into the yards. For a moment there I wanted to turn tail and run back to my sleepy little island.

I soon got over that, thank heavens, and caught a taxi to Chelsea. Terribly extravagant, I know, but I wasn't quite ready to face the tube with all my luggage. I'm just a teensy bit scared of the London Underground.

The driver asked me what district I wanted to go to, and when I told him Chelsea, SW3, he didn't say anything but I could see by the way he blinked that he was impressed. When I got here I was pretty darned impressed, too.

But I'm worried, Patrick.

This isn't exactly an even house swap.

Your place is so gorgeous! Like a four-storey dolls' house. Sorry, I hope that's not offensive to a man. I love it all—the carpeted staircases and beautiful arched windows and marble fireplaces and the bedrooms with their own en suite bathrooms. There's even a bidet! *Blush.* It took me a while to work out what it was. I'd never seen one before.

Meanwhile, you'll be discovering the green tree frogs in my toilet. Gosh, Patrick, can you bear it?

I love the sitting room, with all your books—you're quite a reader, aren't you?—but I think my favourite room is the kitchen, right at the bottom of your house. I love the black and white tiles on the floor and the glass French doors opening onto a little courtyard at the back.

I had my morning cuppa out in the courtyard this morning, sitting in a little pool of pale English sunshine. And there was a tiny patch of daffodils at my feet! I've never seen daffodils growing before.

So many firsts!

After breakfast I went for a walk along the King's Road, and everyone looked so pink-cheeked and glamorous, with their long, double knotted scarves and boots. I bought myself a scarf (won't be able to afford boots). I so wanted to look like all the other girls, but I can't manage the pink cheeks.

I swear I saw a television actor. An older man, don't know his name, but my grandmother used to love him.

But crikey, Patrick. I look around here and I have all this—I feel like I'm living in Buckingham Palace—and then I think about you on the other side of the world in my tiny Pandanus Cottage, which is—well, you'll have seen it for yourself by now. It's very basic, isn't it? Perhaps I should have warned you that I don't even have a flatscreen TV.

Do write and tell me how you are— hopefully not struck dumb with horror.

Cheers, as you Brits say

Molly

To: Patrick Knight <patrick.knight@mymail. com>

From: Molly Cooper <molly.cooper@flower-mail.com>

Subject: Are you there yet?

Sorry to sound like your mother, Patrick, but could you just drop a quick line to let me know you've arrived and you're OK and the house is OK?

M

PS I'm still happy and excited, but I can't believe how cold it is here. Isn't it supposed to be spring?

To: Patrick Knight <patrick.knight@mymail. com>

From: Felicity Knight <flissK@mymail.com>

Subject: Touching base

Hello darling

I imagine you must be in Australia by now. I do hope you had a good flight. I promise I'm not going to bother you the whole time you're away, but I just needed to hear that you've arrived safely and all is well and to wish you good luck again with writing your novel.

Love from the proud mother of a future world-famous, bestselling author.

xx

To: Molly Cooper <molly.cooper@flowermail.com>
From: Patrick Knight <patrick.knight@mymail.com>
Subject: Re: Just checking

Dear Molly

Yes, I'm here, safe and sound, thank you, and everything's fine. It was well worth the twenty-hour flight and crossing the world's hemispheres just to get here. Don't worry. Your house suits my needs perfectly and the setting is beautiful. Everything's spotless, just as you promised, and the new sheets are splendid. Thank you for ironing them.

As I told you, I'm planning to write a book, so I don't need loads of luxury and I don't plan to watch much TV. What I need is a complete change of scenery and inspiration, and the view from your front window provides both.

I've already rearranged the furniture so that I can have a table at the window and take in the fabulous view across the bay to Cape Cleveland. All day long the sea keeps changing colour with the shifting patterns of the sun and the clouds. It's utterly gorgeous.

I'm pleased you've settled in and that you like what you've found, but don't worry about me. I'm enjoying the sunshine and I'm very happy.

Oh, and thanks also for your helpful notes about the fish in the freezer and the pot plants and the washing machine's spin cycle and the geckos. All points duly noted.

Best wishes
Patrick

To: Felicity Knight <flissK@mymail.com>
From: Patrick Knight <patrick.knight@mymail.com>
Subject: Re: Touching base
Hi Mother
Everything's fine, thanks. I'm settled in here and all's well. Will keep in touch. It's paradise down here, so don't worry about me.

Love to you and to Jonathan
Patrick x

Private Writing Journal, Magnetic Island, April 10th

This feels very uncomfortable.

I've never kept any kind of diary, but apparently it's helpful for serious writers to keep a journal of 'free writing'. Any thoughts or ideas are grist for the mill, and the aim is to keep the 'writing muscle' exercised while waiting for divine inspiration.

I wasn't going to bother. I'm used to figures and spreadsheets, to getting results and getting them quickly, and it feels such a waste of effort to dredge up words that might never be used. But after spending an entire day at my laptop staring at 'Chapter One' at the top of a blank page, I feel moved to try something.

I can blame jet-lag for the lack of productivity. I'm sure my muse will kick in after a day or two, but rather than waste the next couple of days waiting for the words to flow, I'm trying this alternative.

So...what to say?

This isn't a test—no one else will be reading it—so I might as well start with the obvious.

It's an interesting experience to move into someone else's house on the other side of the world, and to be surrounded by a completely different landscape and soundtrack, even different smells.

As soon as I found notes from Molly scattered all over the house, I knew I'd arrived in an alien world. A few examples:

Note on a pot plant: Patrick, would you mind watering this twice a week? But don't leave water lying in the saucer, or mosquitoes will breed.

On the fridge door: Help yourself to the fish in the freezer. There's coral trout, queen fish, wahoo and nannygai. Don't be put off by the strange names, they're delicious. Try them on the barbecue. There's a great barbecue recipe book on the shelf beside the stove.

On the lounge wall, beside the light switch: Don't freak if you see small, cute lizards running on the walls. They're geckos—harmless, and great for keeping the insects down.

Beyond the cottage, the plants and trees are nothing like trees at home. Some are much wilder and stragglier, others lusher and thicker, and all seem to grow in the barest cracks of soil between the huge boulders on this headland.

The birds not only look different but they sound totally alien. There's a bright green parrot with a blue head and yellow throat that chatters and screeches. The kookaburra's laugh is hilarious. Another bird lets out a blood-curdling, mournful cry in the night.

Even the light here is a surprise. So bright it takes a bit of getting used to.

God, this is pathetic. I need red wine. I'm not a writer's toenail.

But I can't give up on the first day. Getting this leave was a miracle. I couldn't believe how generous old George Sims was. Such a surprise that he was worried about me 'burning out'.

But now...my writing. I'd always imagined that writing would be relaxing. I'm sure it is once the words really start to come. I'll plug on.

In spite of all the differences here, or perhaps because of them, Molly Cooper's little cottage feels good to me. It's simple, but it has loads of personality and it's almost as if she hasn't really left. It's bizarre, but I feel as if I've actually met her simply by being here and seeing all her things, touching them, using the soap she left (sandalwood, I believe), eating from her dishes, sleeping in her bed under a white mosquito net.

There's a photo of her stuck on the fridge with a magnet shaped like a slice of watermelon. She's with an elderly woman and it says on the back 'Molly and Gran'. It was taken about a year ago, and Gran looks very frail, but Molly has long, light brown curly hair, a pretty smile, friendly eyes, dimples and terrific legs.

Not that Molly's appearance or personality is in any way relevant. I'm never going to meet her in the flesh. Our houses are our only points of connection.

So…a bit more about her house.

I must admit that I was worried that it might be too girlie, a bit too cute with pastel shades, ribbons and bows. The sort of warm and fuzzy place that could lower a man's testosterone overnight. But it's fine. I especially like its rugged and spectacular setting.

The house itself is small—two bedrooms, one bathroom and one big open room for the kitchen, dining and lounge. It's all on one level and it feels strange not going upstairs to bed at night.

Lots of windows and shutters catch the breezes and the views. Loads of candles. You'd think there was no electricity, the way the candles are scattered everywhere, along with pieces of driftwood and shells, and decorative touches of blue.

I wouldn't normally notice colours, but for fear of sounding like a total dweeb I like all Molly's bits of blue—like echoes of the sea and the sky outside. Very restful.

When I leave the house, the island is hot and sultry, but inside it's cool and quiet and... soothing.

After these past years of financial crisis and endless overtime, this place has exactly the kind of vibe I need. I'm glad I told everyone I was going to be out of contact for the next three months. Apart from the odd e-mail from Molly or my mother, there'll be no phone calls. No text messages, no tweets, no business e-mails...

I think I might try the hammock in the mango tree.

To: Patrick Knight <patrick.knight@mymail.com>
From: Molly Cooper <molly.cooper@flower-mail.com>
Subject: Update

Hi Patrick

How are you? I do hope the island is working its magic on you and that the book is flowing brilliantly.

I've begun to explore London (on foot, or

riding in the gorgeous red double-decker buses—takes more time, but I still can't face the Tube), and I'm trying to do as much sightseeing as I can. Turns out most museums in the city of London don't charge any entrance fee, which is awesome.

To make the most of my time here, I've made a few rules for myself.

Rule 1: Avoid other Aussies. I don't want to spend my whole time talking about home. Just shoot me now.

Rule 2: Educate myself about the 'real' London—not just the tourist must-sees, like Buckingham Palace and Trafalgar Square.

Just as an example: yesterday I was walking the streets around here, and I stumbled upon the house where Oscar Wilde lived more than a hundred years ago. Can you imagine how amazing that is for a girl whose neighbours are wallabies and parrots?

I stood staring at Oscar's front window, all choked up, just thinking about the brilliant plays he wrote, and about him living here all through his trial, and having to go to prison simply for being gay.

You're not gay, are you, Patrick? I shouldn't think so, judging by the reading matter on your bookshelves—mostly sporting biographies and finance tomes or spy novels.

Sorry, your reading tastes and sexual preferences are none of my business, but it's hard not to be curious about you. You haven't even left a photo lying around, but I suppose blokes don't bother with photos.

Speaking of photos, I may go to see the Changing of the Guard, but I do not plan to have my picture taken with a man on horseback and an inverted mop on his head.

Rule 3: Fall in love with an Englishman. Actually, it would be helpful if you were gay, Patrick, because then I could have girly chats with you about my lack of a love-life. Now you've seen the island, you'll understand it's not exactly brimming with datable single men. Most of the bachelors are young backpackers passing through, or unambitious drifters.

My secret fantasy (here I go, telling you anyway) is to go out with a proper English gentleman. Let's get real, here—not Prince William or Colin Firth. I can lower my sights—but not too low. Colin Firth's little brother would be acceptable.

After a lifetime on an island where most of the young men spend their days barefoot and wearing holey T-shirts and board shorts, I hanker for a man in a smooth, sophisticated suit.

I'd love to date a nicely spoken Englishman who treats me like a lady and takes me somewhere cultured—to a concert or a play or an art gallery.

A girl can dream. By the way, I've done an internet search and did you know there are six hundred and seventy-three different shows on in London right now? I can't believe it. I'm gobsmacked. Our island has one amateur musical each year.

Patrick, I warned you I might rattle on. I've always tended to put the jigsaw puzzle of my thoughts on paper. For now, I'll leave you in peace.

M

To: Patrick Knight <patrick.knight@mymail.com>
From: Molly Cooper <molly.cooper@flowermail.com>
Subject: Cleaning

Cidalia came today. She's sweet, isn't she? And she speaks very good English. I've never met anyone from Brazil, so we sat at the kitchen table—I wasn't sure how Upstairs/Downstairs you were about entertaining employees in the sitting room—and over a cosy cuppa she told me all about her family and her childhood in San Paolo. So interesting!

But, gosh, Patrick, I didn't realise she was going to continue cleaning your house while I'm here. Apparently you've already paid her in advance. That's kind and thoughtful, and I realise Cidalia wouldn't want to lose her job here, but I haven't arranged for anyone to come and clean my house for you. It didn't even occur to me.

Magnetic Island must feel like a third world country to you.

If you would like a cleaner, I could contact Jodie Grimshaw in Horseshoe Bay. She's a single mum who does casual cleaning jobs, but I'm afraid you'd have to watch her, Patrick. I do feel rather protective of you, and Jodie's on the lookout for a rich husband. Added to that, her child is scarily prone to tantrums.

Do let me know if I can help. I could also try the Sapphire Bay resort. They could probably spare one of their cleaners for one morning a week.

Best
Molly

To: Molly Cooper <molly.cooper@flowermail. com>
From: Patrick Knight <patrick.knight@mymail. com>
Subject: Re: Cleaning

Dear Molly

Thanks for your warning about Jodie G. It came in handy when I met her at the supermarket this morning. She was rather...shall I say, proactive? Your tip-off was helpful.

Actually, I don't need a cleaner, thank you. I've worked out the intricacies of the dustpan and broom, and your house is so compact I can clean it in a jiffy. No doubt you're surprised to hear that I can sweep, even though I'm not gay. ☺ I might even figure out how to plug in the vacuum cleaner soon.

To be honest, the lack of a cleaning woman doesn't bother me nearly as much as the fact that I can't go swimming. Who would have thought you can't swim on a tropical island? Apparently there are deadly jellyfish in the water, and a rogue saltwater crocodile cruising up and down the coastline. All the beaches are closed. And it's stinking hot!

That's my grumble.

For your part, I'm concerned that you're nervous about using the Tube. I can understand it might be intimidating when your main mode of transport has been the island's ferry service, but the Tube is fast and punctual, and Sloane Square station is very close by. Do give it a try.

Regards

Patrick

PS Someone called Boof rang and invited me down to the pub to watch a cane toad race. I looked on the internet and discovered that cane toads are poisonous South American frogs that can grow as big as dinner plates and breed like rabbits. So I guess the races aren't Ascot. Would appreciate any advice/ warnings.

Private Writing Journal, Magnetic Island, April 16th

This journal isn't helping at all. I'm still staring at a blank page.

Any words I've put down are total rubbish. It's so distressing. The ideas for my novel are perfect in my head. I can see the characters, the setting and the action, but when I try to put them on the page everything turns to garbage.

I'm beginning to think that Molly Cooper's a far better writer than I am and she isn't

*even trying. The words just flow from her.
I'm feeling the first flutters of panic. I hate
failure. How did I ever think I could write an
entire novel? It's all in my head, but that's no
use unless I can get it into a manuscript.*

*I'm going for a long hike. Walking is sup-
posed to be very good for writer's block.*

To: Patrick Knight <patrick.knight@mymail.
com>
From: Molly Cooper <molly.cooper@flower-
mail.com>
Subject: Stingers, etc!

Hi Patrick

I'm sorry. I should have warned you about
the marine stingers, and it's a shame about
the crocodile. The good news is the National
Park people will probably catch the croc and
move it up the coast to somewhere safe and
remote, and the stinger season finishes at the
end of April, so it won't be long now before
you're able to swim. You could try the stinger-
proof enclosure over in Horseshoe Bay, but
swimming inside a big net isn't the same, I
suppose.

Just you wait—the island is paradise in late
autumn and early winter. You'll be able to
swim and skin dive to your heart's content.

I'll draw a map of the island and post it to you, showing you where all the best diving reefs are. And do check out the cane toad races. They sound grotesque, but they're actually fun. Listen to Boof. He catches the toads for the races, and maybe he can put you onto a sure thing to win a few dollars.

How's the writing going?

Molly x

To: Patrick Knight <patrick.knight@mymail.com>
From: Molly Cooper <molly.cooper@flower-mail.com>
Subject: Thank you!

Patrick, you darling! Sorry if that sounds too intimate, when we've never actually met, but it's so, so sweet of you to send Discovering London's Secrets. It arrived this morning. You must have organised it over the internet. How thoughtful!

Believe me—I'm deeply, deeply grateful. I've looked at other travel books in the shops, but they only seem to cover all the popular sights, which are fabulous, of course—there's a reason they're popular—but once you've done Piccadilly Circus and Buck Palace, the

Tower and Hyde Park you're hungry for more, aren't you?

Now I'm so well informed I can really explore properly, just the way I'd hoped to. This afternoon I went back to Hyde Park and found the hidden pet cemetery mentioned in this book. It was fascinating, with all those dear little mildewed headstones marking the final resting places of dogs, cats and birds, and even a monkey.

But to use the book you sent properly, I'm going to have to brave the Underground, and that still terrifies me. I hate to think that the whole of London is sitting on top of a network of tunnels and at any given moment there are thousands of people under there, whizzing back and forth in trains.

I do feel ashamed of myself for freaking out like this. I know avoidance only makes these things worse. I'm going to work at getting braver.

M x

To: Molly Cooper <molly.cooper@flowermail. com>
From: Patrick Knight <patrick.knight@mymail. com>
Subject: Re: Thank you!

Hi Molly

Thanks for offering to send a map of the diving spots on the island. It'll be very handy. I'll keep an eye out for the mail van.

So glad you like the book. My pleasure. But, Molly, it does sound as if you're getting yourself very worked up about using the Tube. Of course there are other ways to get around London, but if it's bothering you, and you feel slightly phobic, maybe you need a helping hand?

If you like, I could ask my mother to pop around to No. 34. I know she'd be only too happy to show you the ropes. That's not quite as alarming as it sounds. With me she's extremely bossy, but everyone else claims that she can be very calming.

Best wishes

Chin up!

Patrick

To: Patrick Knight <patrick.knight@mymail. com>

From: Molly Cooper <molly.cooper@flower-mail.com>

Subject: Re: Thank you!

Dear Patrick

Yet again, thank you, but I'm afraid I can't

accept your offer of a visit from your mother. I know it was kindly meant, but I couldn't impose on her like that.

From the way I rabbit on, you probably think I'm very young—but I'm actually twenty-four, and quite old enough to tackle the challenge of catching a train.

I've never liked to play damsel in distress, and, while this fear may be unreasonable, it's something I must conquer on my own.

Sincerely

Molly

PS You haven't mentioned your book. You must be very modest, Patrick. Or does your English reserve prevent you from confiding such personal information to a nosy Aussie?

CHAPTER THREE

Text message from Karli, April 19, 10.40 a.m.:
U never told us yr house swapper is seriously hot.

To: Karli Henderson <hendo86@flowermail.com>
From: Molly Cooper <molly.cooper@flowermail.com>
Subject: House swap

Hi, Karli. Sorry—I can't afford to reply to an international text message, so I'm resorting to e-mail. I must say your text came as a surprise. After all, the whole house swap idea came from you, and you knew I was swapping with a guy called Patrick Knight. As you also know, I only ever saw pictures of his house. I still have no idea what he looks like, so I couldn't tell you anything about his appearance.

Actually, the lack of photos lying about here (not even an album that I can take a sneaky peek at) made me think that Patrick was shy about his appearance.

Is he seriously good-looking?

Honestly?

I'm having a ball here—not on the guy front (sigh), just exploring London. But I'm eventually going to have to get some work. The mortgage must be paid. As you know, Pandanus Cottage is my one and only asset, my key to getting ahead.

Have you spoken to Patrick? Does he have a sexy English accent? I've discovered that not many Londoners actually speak like Jeremy Irons or Colin Firth, which is a bit of a disappointment for me, but I suppose others wouldn't agree. Beauty is in the ear of the receiver, after all.

How's Jimbo?

Molly x

To: Molly Cooper <molly.cooper@flowermail.com>

From: Karli Henderson <hendo86@flowermail.com>

Subject: Re: House swap

Glad you're having a great time, Mozza, but I'm not sure that I should give you too many details about your swapper's looks. You might come racing home.

Be fair, girl. You're over there in London with millions of Englishmen and we have just one here. Not that your Patrick has shown any signs of wanting to mix with the locals. He's a bit aloof. Dare I say snooty? He brushed off Jodie Grimshaw. He was ever so polite, apparently, but even she got the message—and you know what that takes.

Our news is that Jimbo's applying for a job with a boat builder in Cairns, so it could turn out that we won't be on the island for much longer.

Have I told you lately that I'm very proud of you, Molly? I think you're so brave to be living in a huge city on the far side of the world. All alone.

You're my hero. Believe it.

Karli x

To: Karli Henderson <hendo86@flowermail. com>

From: Molly Cooper <molly.cooper@flower-mail.com>

Subject: House swap

Karli, I'm sending positive thoughts to Jimbo for the job interview in Cairns, although I'm sure you know I'm going to really miss you guys if you leave the island. You've been my best friends my whole life!

But I can't be selfish. I know how much you'd like Jimbo to have a steady job that pays well, and you'll be able to start planning your future (including that trip to Vegas), so good luck!!

Re: Patrick Knight. I hope he's not being too standoffish and stuck up, or the islanders will give him a hard time.

I'm sure he's not really snooty. He and I have been swapping e-mails and he seems a bit reserved, but quite nice and helpful. Actually, he's probably keeping to himself because he simply hasn't time to socialise. He's very busy writing a book, and he only has three months off, so he'll have his head down, scribbling (or typing) madly.

Just the same, I think you're mean not telling me more about him. He's in my house, sleeping in my bed. Really, that's a terribly intimate relationship, and yet I have no idea what he looks like!

Why are you holding back? What are you hiding about him? Maybe you could find time to answer a few quick questions?

Is Patrick tall? Yes? No?

Dark? Yes? No?

Young? Like under 35? Yes? No?

Is he muscular? Yes? No?
Good teeth? Yes? No?
All of the above?
None of the above?
M x

To: Molly Cooper <molly.cooper@flowermail.com>
From: Karli Henderson <hendo86@flowermail.com>
Subject: Re: House swap
Chillax, girlfriend.
All of the above.
K

To: Patrick Knight <patrick.knight@mymail.com>
From: Molly Cooper <molly.cooper@flowermail.com>
Subject: FYI

Progress report on the tube assault by Ms Molly Elizabeth Cooper:

A preliminary reconnaissance of Sloane Square Tube station was made this afternoon at 2.00 p.m.

- Thirty minutes were spent in the forecourt, perusing train timetables and observing Londoners purchasing tickets and passing through turnstiles
- Names of the main stations on the yel-

low Circle Line between Sloane Square and King's Cross were memorised—South Kensington, Gloucester Road, Notting Hill Gate, Paddington, Baker Street. Ms Cooper didn't cheat. She loved learning those names and letting them roll off her tongue!

• Ms Cooper acknowledged that people emerging from the Underground did not appear traumatised. Most looked bored, tired or in a dreadful hurry. A handful of passengers almost, but not quite, smiled. One was actually laughing into a mobile phone.

• Ms Cooper purchased a day pass, which she may use some time in the near future.

Ms Cooper's next challenge:

• To actually enter the Underground.

To: Molly Cooper <molly.cooper@flowermail.com>
From: Patrick Knight <patrick.knight@mymail.com>
Subject: Re: FYI

Dear Molly

Congratulations! I'm very proud of you for taking such positive steps. I feared you'd miss another great London experience. In no time you'll be dashing about on the Underground and reading racy novels to conquer your boredom instead of your fear.

Speaking of novels—you've expressed concern about the progress of mine, but I can assure you it is well in hand. It's a thriller, set in the banking world. It has an intricate plot, so I want to plan every twist and turn very carefully in advance. To this end, I've been taking long walks on the island. I walked from Alma Bay to The Forts and back yesterday. A group of Japanese tourists pointed out a lovely fat koala asleep in the fork of a gum tree.

While I'm walking, I think every aspect of my novel through in fine detail. The plotting is almost complete, and I plan to start the actual writing very soon.

Regards
P

To: Patrick Knight <patrick.knight@mymail.com>
From: Molly Cooper <molly.cooper@flowermail.com>
Subject: Re: FYI

That is such a brilliant idea—to set your novel in the banking world. Don't they always say you should write about what you know? And a thriller! Wow! I'd love to hear more.

Go, you!
M x

Private Writing Journal, April 27th.

Working hard or hardly working? Ha-ha-ha-ha-ha-ha.

I'm attacking the novel from a different angle (away from the window—views can be too distracting). I've gone about as far as I can with planning the plot, so I'm creating character charts now. A good story is all about the people in it, so once I have a firm grip on the lead characters the story will spring to life on the page.

Here goes...

Hero: Harry Shooter—*nearing forty, former intelligence officer with MI5, hired by the Bank of England specifically to hunt down spies who pose as bank employees then hack into the systems and siphon off funds. Harry's a tough guy—lean and stoic, hard-headed but immaculately dressed, with smooth, debonair manners. A modern James Bond.*

Female lead: Beth Harper—*mid-twenties. Innocent bank teller. Shoulder-length curly hair, lively smile, great legs, sparkling eyes... Mouthy—and nosy—yet smart...*

That's as far as I've got. For the past half-hour I've been staring out of the frigging window again.

This is hopeless. Writing down a few details

*hasn't helped. I'm no closer to actually start-
ing my novel. I can't just dive into the fun bits,
the action. What I need is to work out first
what these characters would actually say to
each other, how they'd think, how they'd feel!
What I really need is a starting situation—
something that will grab the reader.*

It won't come.

I'm still blocked.

*I have a sickening feeling that this whole
house swapping venture has been a huge,
hideous mistake. The strangeness and new-
ness of everything here is distracting rather
than helpful. I can't concentrate and then I
procrastinate and the cycle continues.*

*I guess this is what happens when you're
desperate and you choose a holiday destination by spinning the globe. Normally I would
have given such a venture much more thought.
Thing is, apart from enjoying the beautiful
scenery on this island there's not a lot else
to do. That was supposed to be a plus.*

*If the writing was flowing everything would
be fine.*

*But if it's not, what have I got? There are
a few cafés and resorts, a pub or two, a gallery here and there, but no cinema. Not even
a proper library.*

I spend far too much of my time thinking about Molly in London, imagining the fun of showing her around, helping her to explore the hidden secrets she's so keen to discover.

Funny, how a stranger can make you take a second look at your home town.

I feel like a fraud.

To: Patrick Knight <patrick.knight@mymail.com>
From: Molly Cooper <molly.cooper@flower-mail.com>
Subject: Rambling

Patrick, would you believe I actually woke up feeling homesick today? I can't believe it. I haven't been here long enough to be homesick, but I looked out the window at the grey skies and the sea of rooftops and streams of people and streets and traffic and fumes and I just longed for my tree-covered headland, where I can't see another house, and to be able to breathe in fresh, unpolluted air.

I stopped myself from moping by going to Wimbledon Common. It involved a bit of jumping on and off buses, but I got there— and it was perfect. Just what I needed with its leafy glades and tangled thickets and stretches of heath. I love that it still has a wild feel and hasn't been all tidied up—and yet it's right in the middle of London.

The minor crisis is over. I'm back in love with your city, Patrick.

Molly x

To: Patrick Knight <patrick.knight@mymail.com>
From: Molly Cooper <molly.cooper@flower-mail.com>
Subject: Your mother...long!

You win, Patrick.

Your mother came, she saw, she conquered. In the nicest possible way, of course. I have now ventured into the bowels of the Underground, I've travelled all the way to Paddington Station and back, and it didn't hurt a bit.

Let me tell you how it happened.

WARNING: this will be a long read, but it's all of your making!

It started with a phone call this morning at about ten o'clock.

'Is that Molly?' a woman asked in a beautiful voice.

I said, tentatively, 'Yes.' I couldn't think who would know me.

'Oh, lovely,' she said. 'I'm so pleased to catch

you at home, Molly. This is Felicity Knight. Patrick's mother.'

I responded—can't remember what I actually said. I was too busy hoping I didn't sound as suddenly nervous as I felt. Your mother's voice is so very refined and my accent is... well, very okker. (Australian!)

She said, 'I have some errands to run this afternoon, and I'll be just round the corner from Alice Grove, so I was hoping I could pop in to say hello.'

'Of course,' I said in my plummiest voice. 'That would be lovely.'

But I could smell a rat, Patrick. Don't think you can fool me. I knew you'd sent her to check up on me—maybe even to hold my hand on the Tube. However, I must admit that even though I told you not to speak to your mum about my little problem I am honestly very grateful that you ignored me.

'We could have afternoon tea,' your mother said.

I tried to picture myself presiding over a tea party. Thank heavens my grandmother taught me how to make proper loose-leaf tea in a teapot, but I've never been one for baking cakes. What else could we eat for afternoon tea?

I shouldn't have worried. Your mum was ten jumps ahead of me.

'There's the loveliest little teashop near you,' she said next. 'They do scrumptious high teas.'

And you know, Patrick, I had the most gorgeous afternoon.

Your mother arrived, looking beautiful. Doesn't she have the most enviable complexion and such elegant silver-grey hair? She was wearing a dove-grey suit, with a lavender fleck through it, and pearls. I was so pleased I'd brought a skirt with me. Somehow it would have been totally Philistine to go to high tea in Chelsea in jeans.

And, you know...normally, beautifully elegant women like your mother can make me feel self-conscious about my untidy curls. My hands and feet seem to grow to twice their usual size and I bump into and break things (like delicate, fine bone china), and I trip on steps, or the edges of carpet.

Somehow, magically, Felicity (she insisted that I mustn't call her Mrs Knight) put me so at ease that I felt quite ladylike. At least I didn't break or spill anything, and I didn't trip once.

We dined in fine style. The tea was served in a silver teapot and we drank from the finest porcelain cups—duck-egg-blue with gold rims and pink roses on the insides—and the dainty food was served on a three-tiered stand.

And, no, I didn't lift my pinkie finger when I drank my tea.

We stuffed ourselves (in the most delicate way) with cucumber sandwiches and scones with jam and clotted cream and the daintiest melt-in-your-mouth pastries.

And we talked. Oh, my, how we talked. Somehow your mother coaxed me to tell her all about myself—how my parents died when I was a baby and how I was raised on the island by my grandmother. I even confessed to my worry that living on an island has made me insular, not just geographically but in my outlook, which is why I'm so keen to travel. And that my first choice was London because my favourite childhood story was *101 Dalmatians*, and I've watched so many movies and read so many books set in London.

And because my father was born here.

I was very surprised when that little bit of info slipped out. It's honestly not something I dwell on. My parents died when I was eighteen months old, and I only have the teensiest memories of them...so wispy and fleeting I'm not sure they're real. I think I can remember being at floor level, fascinated by my mother's painted toenails. And lying in a white cot, watching a yellow curtain flutter against a blue sky. My father's smiling face. My hand in his.

It's not a lot to go on. My gran was the most important person in my life, but she died just under a year ago, and if I think about my missing family too much I start to feel sorry for myself.

But, talking to your mother, I learned that your father lives somewhere up in Scotland now, and you don't see him very much. Why would any sane man divorce Felicity? I'm so glad Jonathan has arrived on the scene. Yes, her new man got a mention, too.

In the midst of our conversation it suddenly felt very important for me to find where my dad was born. I'd like to know something about him, even just one thing. So I'm adding his birthplace to my list of things I want to discover while I'm here, although I'm not quite sure where to start.

You'll be relieved to hear that I stopped myself from telling Felicity about my dream of dating a British gent. A girl has to have some secrets.

It's different talking to you, Patrick. I can tell you such things because we're not face-to-face. You're a safe twelve thousand miles away, so you get to hear everything. You're very tolerant and non-judgemental and I love you for it.

Felicity, of course, told me loads about you, but you know that already, so I won't repeat it. Anyway, you'd only get a swelled head. Your mother adores you—but you know that, too, don't you? And she's so proud that you're writing a novel. You wrote very clever essays at school, so she knows you'll be a huge success.

Anyway, as I was saying, we got on like the proverbial house on fire—so much so that I was shocked when I realised how late it was. Then, as we were leaving, Felicity told me she was catching the Tube home.

That was a shock, Patrick. I'd been lulled into a false sense of security and had totally forgotten the possibility that she might know about my Tube issues. Besides, your mother has such a sophisticated air I assumed she'd catch a taxi if she hadn't brought her own car.

But she said the Tube was fast and convenient, and so I walked with her to Sloane Square Station and we chatted all the way until we were right inside. And then it seemed like the right thing to do to wait with her till her train arrived. Which meant stepping onto the escalator and heading down, down into the black hole of the Underground!

That was a seriously freaking-out moment.

Honestly, I could feel the beginnings of a panic attack, and I was sure I couldn't breathe. But Felicity was so calm and smiling, telling me what a lovely afternoon she'd had, and suggesting that maybe we could have another afternoon together some time. She made me feel so OK I managed to start breathing again.

I must admit that once I was down there, standing on the platform, the station seemed so very big and solid and well-lit and I felt much better than I'd expected to. I actually told Felicity then that I'd been a tiny bit frightened, and she said she totally understood; she would be terrified if she was in the Australian Outback, and why didn't I travel with her to Paddington?

She had to change trains there, but if I felt OK I could travel back on my own, and I'd soon be a Tube veteran. She even gave me her mobile phone number in case I got into trouble. She wouldn't have reception until she was above ground again, but it didn't matter—I was over the worst by then, and actually sitting on the train was fine.

Everything went so well I was able to text her: *Thanks. This is a breeze!*

So I think I'm cured.

And I know that ultimately you're the person I should thank, Mr Patrick Knight-in-shining-armour. Because you arranged it, didn't you?

I wish there was some way I could help you, but I don't know the first thing about writing a novel.

Molly

XXXXXXXXXXXXXXXXXXXXXXXXXXX

PS Feel free to tell me to pull my head in, but I did wonder if it's possible to over-think the planning of a book. The way I over-thought the whole business of entering the Tube. Do you ever get the urge to just leap right in and let the words flow?

CHAPTER FOUR

To: Patrick Knight <patrick.knight@mymail.com>
From: Felicity Knight <flissK@mymail.com>
Subject: Mission accomplished

Dear Patrick

It's a pity you're on the other side of the world and unable to carry out your own rescue mission.

I only say this because Molly Cooper is charming, and I thoroughly enjoyed a highly entertaining afternoon with her. It seems to me that your taste in women improves considerably when you change your selection criteria. Perhaps you should try choosing your girlfriends by their houses.

Molly may not be a pint-size blonde, as most of your girlfriends are, but she can hold up her end of a conversation. She's very smart, Patrick, and you should see the way her blue eyes sparkle. They're breathtaking.

Darling, thank you for sending me on a very pleasant errand. I must say I was very curious about the girl you'd swapped houses with. Now that curiosity is happily satisfied.

I hope you're having as much fun with writing your novel as Molly seems to be having here in London.

Love
Mother xx

Private Writing Journal, Magnetic Island, April 30th

Note about character development: it might work quite well if I give my heroine a private fear that she must overcome.

To: Molly Cooper <molly.cooper@flowermail. com>
From: Patrick Knight <patrick.knight@mymail. com>
Subject: Re: Thank you!

Hi Molly

Your map of the island's reefs arrived today. Thanks so much. The information will be very helpful, and your request that I don't show the location of these reefs to too many tourists was duly noted. I'm honoured that you're sharing some of your island's secrets with me, a mere visitor.

I also enjoyed very much your drawings of the coral fish and the other weird and wonderful creatures that I'm likely to encounter when I finally enter the Pacific Ocean.

Your artistic efforts made me smile. Have you ever thought of a new career as a cartoonist?

I'm very keen to see a Chelmon rostratus (thank you for the helpful labels). Those fish are gorgeous, with their bright black, yellow and white stripes and their long snouts. And I'm fascinated by the anemone fish.

You were right about the crocodile. He was caught in Florence Bay—six brave fellows from the National Park manhandled him, trussed him up like a giant Christmas turkey and relocated him further north. Apparently he won't come back this way now that we're approaching the winter. Thank God.

So I can't wait to start diving. You've certainly whetted my appetite for discovering *what lies beneath*....

Molly, I'm very pleased to hear that you've got the Tube business sorted. I know my mother enjoyed meeting you. Well done.

It's getting a little cooler here at last. Today

it's hard to believe it's autumn. The temperatures are almost down to those of an English summer's day.

If you'd like any help with looking for your father's birthplace, do sing out.

Best
Patrick

To: Molly Cooper <molly.cooper@flowermail.com>
From: Patrick Knight <patrick.knight@mymail.com>
Subject: PS

Molly, another thought. You might be surprised to know that you could quite possibly help me with this novel by sharing your reactions to London.

You were worried about sending me extra-long messages but I've enjoyed the descriptions in your e-mails...and I've found them helpful.

I'm still learning the ropes, so to speak, and it would be extremely useful to see my home town described through a fresh pair of eyes. In fact your reactions to life in general could be helpful, as it's hard for a fellow to get inside the female mind. In other words, feel free to continue sharing your discoveries and insights. Positive or negative—you won't hurt my feelings.

Just if the whim takes you.

Warmest wishes

Patrick

To: Patrick Knight <patrick.knight@mymail. com>

From: Molly Cooper <molly.cooper@flower-mail.com>

Subject: My London eye

Dear Patrick

I'm more than happy to rattle on to you about my London adventures, and please feel free to use anything I say in your novel. Wow! What an honour.

I've been thinking that writing must be a lonely occupation, so I can imagine you'd enjoy getting e-mails at the end of a long day at the keyboard.

But if I get too carried away, flooding you with too much information, please tell me.

I had to laugh at a sign I saw today in a Tube station: *A penalty fare will be charged to any passenger who fails to hide true emotions fully or makes any attempt to engage with other passengers.*

That is so what it's like. I do love the way the British poke fun at themselves.

Yesterday I spent the loveliest morning checking out the Kensington Roof Gardens. They're gorgeous. Have you been there? It's amazing—one and a half acres of trees and plants growing thirty metres above Kensington High Street and divided into three lovely themed gardens.

There's an English woodland (which I think might be my favourite), with curving lawns and surprisingly large trees, a stream and little bridges, even a lake with ducks and pink flamingos. I'm so glad it's spring, because there were also lovely flowers everywhere, but unfortunately I don't know their names.

There's also a Tudor garden, with a courtyard and creeper-covered walls and brick paths laid in a herringbone pattern. It's filled with fragrant flowers—lilies, roses and lavender. And the Spanish garden is very dramatic, with its stunning white walls. Apparently it's inspired by the Alhambra in Spain.

By the way, thanks so much for offering to help with my family history research. My grandmother kept a box of papers that belonged to my parents, including their marriage certificate. When I was younger I used to take it out often and read every word. I haven't done that for ages, but I'm almost certain I re-

member that my father was born in Clapham.
I used to want to call it Clap-ham. I know the
year he was born was definitely 1956.

Molly

PS Would you like to send me a list of questions that might help you with getting inside
your female character's head?

To: Molly Cooper <molly.cooper@flowermail.
com>
From: Patrick Knight <patrick.knight@mymail.
com>
Subject: Questions

It's very generous of you to offer to help with
my female character. I hesitate to make these
kinds of demands on your time, but authors
do need to know an awful lot about what's
going on inside their characters, and I'd truly
appreciate your input.

My heroine is Beth Harper and she's a bank
teller, about your age, and I'm supposed to
know about her likes and dislikes—her favourite kinds of clothes and jewellery, favourite
colour, music, animal, etc; her least favourite
of these; her spending habits; her most prized
possession; her talents (piano player, juggler,
poet?); nervous habits. Any thoughts along
those lines would be welcomed.

I'm hoping to create a girl who feels real and unique.

So…whenever you have time…

Gratefully

Patrick

PS If you could tell me your father's full name, I just might have the right contacts to do a little research for you.

To: Patrick Knight <patrick.knight@mymail.com>
From: Molly Cooper <molly.cooper@flower-mail.com>
Subject: Re: Questions

Patrick, I feel like I'm always thanking you, but the very thought of finding out more about my father makes me feel quite wobbly with excitement and emotion, so thank you so much for offering to help. His name was Charles Torrington Cooper, which I think sounds rather dignified, but I'm told that in Australia he was only ever known as Charlie Cooper.

You will no doubt already know what he looked like as there's a photo of him and my mother on my bedside table. You can see that he's to blame for my brown curly hair, but don't you think he has the nicest smile?

Now, about your book. I have to warn you, Patrick, that if you want your character to be unique, I may not be your woman. Truth is, I'm careful and conservative—as ordinary as oatmeal. And, whatever you do, don't give Beth Harper my hair.

Also, my favourite clothes—a bikini and a sarong—might not ring true for a teller in a bank in London.

So last night I sat down and tried to pretend I was Beth and to answer your questions as if I was her—and I suddenly understood your dilemma. It's really, really hard to just make someone up, isn't it? But it's fun, too.

So let's see. If I was Beth, working in a bank, I think I'd be super-prim like a librarian during the day, but I'd wear sexy lingerie underneath my work clothes (to remind the reader of my wild side and because it feels so lovely against my skin). And I'd wear wild colours on my weekends—rainbow-coloured leggings or knee-high red boots with micro-miniskirts. And I'd be the queen of scarves—silk, crocheted, long, short. For when it's cold I'd have a coat with a big faux fur collar.

I'm getting carried away, aren't I? But it's so much fun to pretend to be English. I don't get to wear any of that sort of gear on the island.

Beth's favourite colour would change every week, and her spending habits would be a perfect balance between thriftiness and recklessness—because she wants to enjoy life, but she's also a sensible bank teller. Unlike me. I'm always the same about money—as penny-pinching as they come. I have to be.

Beth's most prized possession is the ridonkulously expensive little red (not black) dress that she bought for the one time she went to the Royal Opera House at Covent Garden with the man of her dreams. (My most prized possession is my house. As I'm sure yours must be for you, Patrick.)

In case you were wondering, my grandmother left Pandanus Cottage to me, but she left me a mortgage, too, because she had to refinance to keep me through the high school years. She sent me to a good private school she couldn't really afford, the darling.

I consider myself very lucky. My house is my ticket to a safe and steady future, so I pay my mortgage rather than splashing out on trendy fashions. That's where living on the island comes in handy. You must have noticed that it's a budget-friendly, fashion-free zone. Anything goes.

Not so for Beth.

Now for her talents. Could she be secretly brilliant at doing arithmetic in her head? (Again, that's the very opposite of me. The calculator on my mobile phone is my best friend.) Could Beth's cleverness be of huge save-the-day importance at some time in your plot?

As for nervous habits… Well, I tend to mess with my hair…as if it wasn't already messy enough. I don't think Beth should do that. I'm positive she has very sleek, flowing hair—the kind of shiny waterfall hair you see in shampoo advertisements. The kind of hair I used to pray for when I was twelve.

Could Beth be a stutterer instead? Could she have worked hard to overcome her stutter, and now it only breaks out when she's really, really nervous—like when your bad guy holds a gun to her head, or, to her huge embarrassment, when really, really gorgeous men speak to her?

Hmm… That's about all I can think of for now. Not sure how helpful any of this might be, but it was fun playing at being an author. There must be times when you feel like a god.

Molly x

PS Patrick, you do know Beth must have a tattoo, don't you? Where it is on her body and what it looks like I'll leave to your fertile authorly imagination.

To: Patrick Knight <patrick.knight@mymail.com>

From: Molly Cooper <molly.cooper@flowermail.com>

Subject: Gainfully employed

You've been very quiet, Patrick. Is everything OK?

I have sad news. I landed a job yesterday and I have to start soon. I'll be serving drinks behind the bar in the Empty Bottle—which, as you know, is a newly renovated pub just around the corner. Four evenings a week. But that still leaves me with mornings free, and three full days each week for sightseeing.

I admit I'm not looking forward to working, but the coffers need bolstering, and at least this job should provide great opportunities to meet loads of new people (maybe even that dream man). I can't complain about a few shifts behind a bar when you're spending the whole time you're away slaving over a hot laptop.

I hope the novel is going really well for you.

Best wishes

Molly

To: Molly Cooper <molly.cooper@flowermail.com>

From: Patrick Knight <patrick.knight@mymail.com>

Subject: Re: Gainfully employed

Thanks for the description of your vision of Beth. I really like it. I think my hero's going to like her, too.

I'm very sorry you have to start work. Seems a pity when there's so much of London you want to see. I guess the extra cash will be helpful, though. Perhaps it will allow you to take a few trips out into the countryside as well? Rural England is very pretty at this time of year.

I've only been in the Empty Bottle on a couple of occasions (my usual is closer to work), but it seemed like a nice pub.

Please keep me informed. It could be a place frequented by the likes of Beth Harper, so keep a lookout for high-heeled red boots and micro-mini-skirts.

I've taken your advice and kitted my heroine out in sexy underwear and your recommended wardrobe.

I'm still giving deep thought to her (discreet) tattoo.

P.

To: Patrick Knight <patrick.knight@mymail.com>
From: Molly Cooper <molly.cooper@flowermail.com>
Subject: A bedtime story

Goldilocks Revisited

So I trudged home late last night, after a gruelling shift at the Empty Bottle. My head was aching from the pub's loud music and all the laughter and shouting of noisy drinkers. In fact my head hurt so much I thought the top might lift right off. As you might imagine, I wasn't in a very good mood.

My mood wasn't improved when I dragged my weary bones into my/your bedroom and switched on the light.

Someone was sleeping in my/your bed!

Someone blonde, naked and busty. And tipsy. Quite tipsy.

You remember Angela, don't you, Patrick?

She'd been at a party a few blocks away and she'd had too much to drink and needed somewhere to crash. She had a key to your house, and I don't think she had to go to a bank to get it from a safety deposit box.

I slept in the spare room, but the bed wasn't made up and I had to go hunting for sheets and blankets. I was so tired I might have slept on top of the satin quilt with only my denim jacket for warmth if satin wasn't so slippery.

Next day, a shade before midday, Angela came downstairs, wrapped in your port wine silk dressing gown and looking somewhat the worse for wear, and she asked about break-fast as if I was a servant.

Patrick, you asked for my reactions to your world, but I suppose I may be coming across as somewhat manipulative in this situation— as if I'm trying to make you feel awkward and maybe even sorry for me. Or you might even think it's the green-eyed monster raising its ugly head. But I'm not the type to get jealous of your former girlfriend when I haven't even met you.

I just don't do headaches well. That's all.

Anyway, I was determined to be generous, so I cooked up an enormous hangover break-fast for Angela and she wolfed it down. Bacon, eggs and tomatoes, with toast and expensive marmalade, plus several cups of strong cof-fee. It all disappeared with the speed of light. The colour came back into her face. She even managed to smile.

I do admit that Angela is exceptionally pretty when she smiles—a beautiful, delicate, silky blonde. I tried to dislike her, but once she understood my reasons for taking up resi-dence in your house—that it was a fair swap and very temporary—she thawed a trillion de-grees.

So then we poured ourselves another mug

of coffee each and settled down to a lovely gossipy chat. About you.

I promise I didn't ask Angela to talk about you, Patrick, but your lovely kitchen is very chat-friendly, and she was the first English girl of my age that I'd had a chance to gossip with. I'd like to think of it more as a cross-cultural, deep and meaningful exchange.

Angela even flipped through the photos on her mobile phone to see if she still had one of you, but you've been deleted, I'm afraid. She told me that she's just one in a string of your neglected girlfriends, and that your work has always, *always* come first.

Case in point—the time you missed her birthday because you had to fly to Zurich (on a weekend). And there were apparently a lot of broken dates and times when you sent last-minute apologies via text messages because you had to work late, when she'd already spent a fortune on having her hair and nails done, and having her legs, and possibly other bits, waxed.

It's not for me to judge, of course.

Maybe Angela (and those other girls who preceded her) should have been more understanding and patient. Maybe you have a very ambitious and driven personality and you can't help working hard. After all, you're using your holidays to write a novel when most people lie on the beach and read novels that other people have written.

Or maybe, just maybe, you could be a teensy bit more thoughtful and considerate and take more care to nurture your personal relationships.

OK, that's more than enough from me. I'm ducking for cover now.

Cheerio!

Molly x

PS Angela was thoughtful enough to return your key.

To: Molly Cooper <molly.cooper@flowermail. com>
From: Patrick Knight <patrick.knight@mymail. com>
Subject: Re: A bedtime story

Dear Molly

I confess I'd completely overlooked the possibility that Angela Carstairs might still have a door key. I'm sorry you were inconvenienced by her unexpected visit, and thanks so much for going above and beyond. You're a good sport, Molly, and I'm very grateful. I'm sure Angela is too.

I suppose I should also thank you for your

feedback and your advice regarding my previous and possible future relationships. As I said before, it's always helpful to receive a fresh perspective.

On the subject of unexpected visitors and questionable relationships, however, you've had a visitor, too. A young man called in here yesterday. A Hell's Angel look-alike with a long red beard and big beefy arms covered in tattoos. He asked ever so politely about some ladies' lingerie which you, apparently, are holding here for him.

I would have been happy to oblige your boyfriend. I might have asked a few pertinent questions. But he seemed very secretive, almost furtive, and I got the distinct impression that he would not welcome my curiosity. As you might imagine I was somewhat at a loss. I had no idea where I could lay my hands on lingerie in his size. I suggested he call back in a few days. Do you have any suggestions or instructions, Molly?

Kindest regards
Patrick

To: Patrick Knight <patrick.knight@mymail.com>
From: Molly Cooper <molly.cooper@flower-mail.com>

Subject: Re: A bedtime story

Wipe that smirk off your face right now, Patrick Knight. I know what you're thinking, and stop it. That visitor was not my boyfriend, and he's certainly not a cross-dresser.

His name is David Howard and he's a butcher in Horseshoe Bay, married to a doting wife with three kids and as straight as a Roman road. But he also has a fabulous singing voice, and he's landed a major role in the local production of *The Rocky Horror Show*. It's all very top secret (and believe me, keeping a secret on Magnetic Island is a big call.) I organised his costume before I left, but I was so busy getting the house ready for you that I forgot to drop it off with the Amateur Players.

I'm sorry David had to disturb you. It's entirely my fault. I left the costume in a black plastic bag on the table next to my sewing machine in the back bedroom, so I'd be very grateful if you could pass it on to him, with my apologies.

Can you imagine the impact and the surprise when big David, covered in tattoos, steps onto the stage?

Thanks!

Molly

To: Molly Cooper <molly.cooper@flowermail.com>

From: Patrick Knight <patrick.knight@mymail.com>

Subject: One parcel of lingerie duly delivered.

Curiosity drove me to take a peek at the lingerie before I handed it over to David, and I must say you sew a very fine seam. The lace on the suspender belts is very fetching.

But while you wriggled off that hook quite neatly, Molly, I can't let you get away completely. You've had another visitor (dare I say admirer?) who turned up here late yesterday afternoon, expecting a massage. Probably the fittest looking character I've seen in a long while. He seemed very upset when I told him your services would not be available till the end of June.

Explain away that one, Miss Molly.

And while I'm on the subject of the men in your life, the strapping young ranger who supervised the crocodile capture last week was very keen to know when you'd be back.

Rest assured, I don't plan to sit down with these fellows for a 'cosy chat', so I won't be passing on any advice to you re: your previous or future relationships.

Patrick

To: Patrick Knight <patrick.knight@mymail. com>

From: Molly Cooper <molly.cooper@flower-mail.com>

Subject: Re: One parcel of lingerie duly delivered

Patrick, I'm sorry. My friends do seem to be interrupting you lately. The guy who turned up for a massage was Josh. But honestly, it's not that kind of massage. He's a footballer—he plays for the local rugby league team and he has a problem with his shoulders. Like a lot of islanders he bucks the system and has no medical insurance, so he balks at handing over money for a professional massage from a physio.

That's why he comes to me.

I massage his shoulders. Only. He keeps me supplied with fish. Hence my well-stocked freezer. As for Max, the crocodile wrangler, I have no idea why he was asking about me. I should think that's nothing more than idle curiosity.

Anyway, as you know, it's not Australian men I'm interested in. I'm still on the lookout for my lovely Englishman. Any advice on where I should hang out to have the best chance of meeting my dream man would be deeply appreciated.

By the way, I've bought a Travelcard and I've done heaps of travelling on the Tube now. On my last day off I went to Piccadilly Circus, to explore the hidden courts and passages of St James's. I found the most amazing, ancient, hidden pub in Ely Street. It's so tiny and dark and dingy and old, and it has the stump of a cherry tree that Elizabeth I danced around!

I was rather overcome just trying to wrap my head around all the history contained in those tiny rooms.

Molly x

PS I'm such a traveller now. Last night, as I was drifting off to sleep, I kept hearing a voice saying, 'Mind the gap.'

To: Patrick Knight <patrick.knight@mymail. com>
From: Felicity Knight <flissK@mymail.com>
Subject: Surprise news

Dearest Patrick

I have the most amazing news. Jonathan has asked me (again) to marry him, and this time I've said yes.

Can you believe it? Your mother is getting married and she couldn't be happier.

As you know, it's taken me a very long time to get over the divorce. Actually, it's taken us both a long time, hasn't it? I know that's so, Patrick, even though you won't give in and talk about it.

I honestly thought I couldn't face another marriage after the way the last one ended, but Jonathan has been such a darling—so patient and understanding.

This time when he proposed I knew it was a case of saying yes or losing him. A man's pride can only take so many knock-backs.

Suddenly (thank heavens) the scales fell from my eyes and I understood without a shadow of a doubt that I couldn't bear to lose him. I simply couldn't let him go.

Now that decision's made such a weight has lifted from my heart. I'm giddy with happiness.

It's all happening in a frightful hurry, though. I think poor Jonathan is terrified that I might change my mind. I won't, of course. I know that as certainly as I know my own name.

So it's to be a May wedding, and then a honeymoon in Tuscany. Have you ever heard of anything more romantic?

Now, darling, I'm including your invitation as an attachment, but Jonathan and I know this writing time is precious to you. You've worked far too hard these past couple of years, and I'm so pleased you've taken this break, so we'll understand perfectly if you can't tear yourself away from your novel. The wedding will be a very small affair. We were lucky enough to book the church after a cancellation.

Even if you can't make it, I know you'll be happy for me.

Oceans of love

Your proud and very happy mother xxx

Patrick Knight
The pleasure of your company is requested
at the marriage of
Felicity Knight
and
Jonathan Langley
on Saturday 21st May
at St Paul's Church, Ealing
at 2.00 p.m.
and afterwards at 3 Laburnum Lane,
West Ealing

To: Felicity Knight <flissK@mymail.com>
From: Patrick Knight <patrick.knight@mymail.com>
Subject: Re: Surprise news

Wow! What fabulous and very welcome news! I'm thrilled, and I know you and Jonathan will be blissfully happy.

You deserve so much happiness, Mother. That's been my main concern ever since Dad left us.

I can just imagine Jonathan's relief. I know he's mad about you, and tying the knot will put him out of his agony.

Your plans sound wonderfully spontaneous and romantic. I'm glad you're just getting on with it and not worrying too much about my presence. That said, I'd love to come back for a quick weekend to join the nuptial celebrations, so I'll give it serious thought and let you know very soon.

Don't fret about my attitude towards my father. I still can't forgive him for what he did to you, but Jonathan's made up for his behaviour in spades.

Love and best wishes to you both
Patrick

Private Writing Journal, Magnetic Island, May 3rd

This isn't about writing...but my mind's churning and it might help to get my thoughts down.

I hate myself for hesitating to jump on a plane and hurry back for my mother's wedding, especially as I wouldn't have stalled if the book had been falling into place.

I've tried to breathe life into the damn thing. I've even tried Molly's suggestion of leaping in and simply letting the writing flow. It worked for two days, then I made the mistake of re-reading what I'd written.

Utter drivel.

And now, of course, I can't stop thinking about my father and what a fool he was to leave my mother and take off with his secretary. His actions were a comical cliché to outsiders looking on, and a truly hurtful shock for us.

I was eighteen at the time, and I'll never forget how shattered my mother was. I wanted to help her, but I knew there was absolutely nothing I could say or do to heal her pain. I bought a plane ticket to Edinburgh, planning to go after my father and—

I never was quite sure what I'd do when I found him. Break his stupid, arrogant nose, I suppose. But Mother guessed what I'd planned and she begged me not to go. Begged me with tears streaming down her face.

So I gave up that scheme, but I was left with so many questions.

Along with everyone else who knew my parents, I could never understand why he did it—apart from the obvious mid-life crisis which had clearly fried his brains. Actually, I do know that my father worried about ageing more than most. He could never stand to waste time, and he hated the idea of his life rushing him towards its inevitable end. Perhaps it's not so very surprising that he started chasing after much younger women.

Fool. I still don't see how he could turn his back on Mother. Everyone loves her. Molly's response to meeting her was the typical reaction of anyone who meets her.

Of course the one thing in this that I've totally understood was my mother's reluctance to enter a second marriage. She didn't want to be hurt again, and my father is to be entirely blamed for that.

But her heart is safe in Jonathan Langley's hands. He's exactly like Molly Cooper's dream man—a charming Englishman, a gentleman to the core—and he and my mother share a deep affection that makes the rest of us envious....

I wonder if Mother wants me to write to tell Dad. She would never ask outright.

To be honest, I don't think I want him to know until Jonathan's ring is safely on her finger and she's away in Italy with him. Maybe I'm being overly cautious, but I'm not going to risk any chance that Dad might turn up and somehow spoil this for her.

To: Patrick Knight <patrick.knight@mymail. com>
From: Molly Cooper <molly.cooper@flowermail.com>
Subject: Impossible dreams

I assume from your silence that you're not going to pass on any wise advice about how I might find my dream Englishman.

Patrick, have you any idea how hard it is?

I don't mean it's hard to get myself asked out—that's happened quite a few times already—but the chaps haven't been my cup of tea. My question is—would you believe how hard it is to find the right style of man?

I've taken some comfort from reading that a clever academic has worked out that finding the perfect partner is only one hundred times more likely than finding an alien. I read it in the Daily Mail on the Tube. See how much progress I've made?

The thing is, I'm not looking for the perfect life partner—just the perfect date. One night is all I ask. But even that goal is depressingly difficult to achieve.

Some people—most people—would say I'm too picky, and of course they'd be right. My dream of dating an English gentleman is completely unrealistic. Mind you, my definition of 'gentleman' is elastic. He doesn't have to be from an upper class family.

I'm mainly talking about his manners and his clothes and—well, yes, his voice. I do adore a plummy English accent.

I know it's a lot to ask. I mean, if such a man existed why would he be interested in a very ordinary Australian girl?

I know my expectations are naive. I know I should lower my sights. This maths geek from the newspaper has worked out that of the thirty million women in the UK, only twenty-six would be suitable girlfriends for him. The odds would be even worse for me, a rank outsider.

Apparently, on any given night out in London, there is a 0.0000034 per cent chance of meeting the right person.

That's a 1 in 285,000 chance.

You'd have better odds if you went to the cane toad races, Patrick. Of winning some money, I mean, not finding the perfect date.

But then you're not looking for an island romance. Are you?

Molly

CHAPTER FIVE

To: Molly Cooper <molly.cooper@flowermail. com>
From: Patrick Knight <patrick.knight@mymail. com>
Subject: Re: Impossible dreams

Molly, I hesitate to offer advice on how to engineer a date with the kind of man you're looking for, because in truth I'm not sure it's a good idea. I hate to be a wet blanket, but I'm more inclined to offer warnings. The sad fact is that a public school accent and your idea of 'gentlemanly' manners may not coincide.

Of course there are always exceptions. And you might be lucky. But don't expect that any man who speaks with Received Pronunciation and wears an expensive three-piece suit will behave like a perfect gentleman. When you're alone with him, that is.

Sorry. I know that's a grim thing to say about my fellow countrymen, but I do feel respon-

sible, and I'd hate you to be upset. All I can honestly say is take care!
Sincerely
Patrick

To: Molly Cooper <molly.cooper@flowermail. com>
From: Patrick Knight <patrick.knight@mymail. com>
Subject: Cane toad races

You've been unusually quiet lately, Molly, and I find myself worrying (like an anxious relative) that something's happened. I'd hate to think I've crushed your spirit. I suspect I knocked a ruddy great hole in your dating dreams, but I hope I haven't completely quelled your enthusiasm for adventure and romance.

I trust you're simply quiet because you're having a cracking good time and you're too busy to write e-mails.

However, in an effort to cheer you up (if indeed you are feeling low), I thought I'd tell you about my experiences at the toad races the night before last. Yes, I've been, and you were right—I enjoyed the evening. In fact, I had a hilarious time.

As you've no doubt guessed, I wasn't really looking forward to going, but I desperately needed a break from my own company and decided to give the cane toads a try.

I'd been curious about how these races were set up, and why they've become such a tourist draw. I'd read that the toads are considered a pest here. They were brought out to eat beetles in the sugar cane, but they completely ignored the beetles and killed all sorts of other wildlife instead. They ate anything smaller than themselves, and they poisoned the bigger creatures that tried to eat them.

I was a bit worried that if cane toads are considered a pest the races might be cruel, so I was relieved to discover that, apart from having a number stuck on their backs and being kept in a bucket until the race starts, the toads don't suffer at all.

The mighty steeds racing last night were:
1. Irish Rover
2. Prince Charles
3. Herman the German
4. Yankee Doodle
5. Italian Stallion
6. Little Aussie Battler

By the time all the toads were safely under a bucket in the centre of the dance floor, and the race was ready to start, there was quite a noisy and very international crowd gathered. Naturally I had to put my money on Prince Charles.

A huge cheer went up when the bucket was lifted and the toads took off.

At least the Italian Stallion took off. The other toads all seemed a bit stunned, and just sat there blinking in the light. I yelled and cheered along with the noisiest punters, but I'd completely given up hope for my Prince Charlie when he suddenly started taking giant leaps.

What a roar there was then (especially from me)! You have no idea. Well, actually, you probably do have a very good idea. As you know, the first toad off the dance floor wins the race, and good old Prince Charles beat the Italian Stallion by a whisker. No, make that a wart.

There'd been heavy betting on the Australian and American toads, so I won quite a haul—a hundred dollars—and the prize money was handed over with a surprising degree of ceremony. I was expected to make a speech.

I explained that I was a banker from London and, as a gesture, I wanted to compensate for the unsatisfactory exchange rate as quickly as possible by converting my winnings into cold beer.

That announcement brought a huge cheer.

The cheering was even louder when I added that if everyone would like to come up to my place (that is, Molly Cooper's place) there'd be a celebratory party starting very shortly.

Everyone came, Molly. I hope you don't mind. We all squeezed in to your place and had a fabulous night. I lit every single one of your candles and Pandanus Cottage looked sensational. It did you proud.

The party went on late.

Very.

I do hope you're having a good time, too.

Warmest wishes

Patrick x

To: Patrick Knight <patrick.knight@mymail.com>
From: Molly Cooper <molly.cooper@flowermail.com>
Subject: Re: Cane toad races

Dear Patrick

That's great news about the cane toad races and the party. I was worried that, working so much by yourself, you might have given the islanders the impression you were a bit aloof. Clearly that's not so.

I'm afraid I haven't been up to partying in recent days. I'm laid low with a heavy cold, so I've been curled up at home, sipping hot lemon drinks and watching daytime television. Cidalia's been a darling. She's come in every day to check on me and make these lemon drinks, and a divine chicken soup which she calls canja.

She said it was her grandmother's cure-all—which is interesting, because it's almost the same as the soup my gran used to make for me. Seems that chicken soup is an international cure-all.

But that's not all, Patrick. Your mother telephoned while my cold was at its thickest and croakiest, and when she heard how terrible I sounded she sent me a gift box from...

Harrods!

Can you believe it? I was so stunned. It's a collection of gorgeous teas—Silver Moon, English Breakfast, Earl Grey—all in individual cotton (note that: cotton, not paper) teabags. Such a luxury for me, and so kind of her. But how can I ever repay her?

As you can see, I've been very well looked after, and I'm on the mend again now, and cheered by your account of your adventures at the toad races. I'm trying to picture you cheering madly and delivering your tongue-in-cheek speech. Fantastic.

I'm more than happy that you hosted a party at my place. The candles do make the little cottage look quite romantic, don't they? And with all that beer, and with you as host, I'm not surprised people wanted to stay. I bet I can guess who crashed and was still there next morning.

And I'm also betting that you heard Jodie Grimshaw's entire life story at around 2.00 a.m. Looks like you're really settling in, Patrick. That's great.

Oh, thanks for your advice re: English gentlemen, but don't worry. Your warnings didn't upset me—although they weren't really necessary either. I might sound totally naive, but I did see the way Hugh Grant's character behaved in Bridget Jones, and I have good antennae. I can sense a jerk at fifty paces.

Best wishes
Molly

To: Felicity Knight <flissK@mymail.com>
From: Patrick Knight <patrick.knight@mymail.com>

Subject: Many thanks

Dear Mother

I'm sure Molly's already thanked you for sending a gift box when she was ill, but I want to thank you, too. As you know, Molly's totally on her own in the world. She puts on a brave face, but she was very touched by your thoughtfulness, and so was I.

Love

P

To: Molly Cooper <molly.cooper@flowermail.com>

From: Karli Henderson <hendo86@flowermail.com>

Subject: Your house swapper

Hi Molly

It's Jodie here, using Karli's e-mail. I'm helping her to pack because she and Jimbo are heading off to Cairns. I just thought you might be interested to know that your house swapper Patrick is totally hot and throws the best parties evah. Oh, man. That party last Saturday night was totally off the chain.

Bet you wish you were here.

Jodie G

To: Karli Henderson <hendo86@flowermail.com>
From: Molly Cooper <molly.cooper@flower-mail.com>
Subject: Hands off, Jodie

Sorry, Jodie, I'm going to be blunt. Patrick Knight is not for you. He's—

The message *Subject: Hands off, Jodie* **has not been sent. It has been saved in your drafts folder.**

To: Molly Cooper <molly.cooper@flowermail.com>
From: Karli Henderson <hendo86@flower-mail.com>
Subject: So long, farewell, *auf wiedersehen*, etc.

Hi Molly

I'm afraid this is going to be my last e-mail. What with the move and everything, Jimbo and I are a bit strapped for cash, so I've sold this computer, along with half our CDs, in a garage sale. This is my last e-mail to anyone, and I won't be back online for some time, but I'm sure things will improve once we're settled in our new jobs in Cairns. Will be thinking of you, girlfriend. Have a blast in London.

Love
Karli xxxxxxxxx

To: Molly Cooper <molly.cooper@flowermail.com>

From: Patrick Knight <patrick.knight@mymail.com>

Subject: An address in Clapham

Molly, my (secret) contacts at the bank have found a Charles Torrington Cooper, born in 1956, who used to live at 16 Rosewater Terrace, Clapham.

I can't guarantee that this is your father, but Torrington is an unusual middle name, and everything else matches, so chances are we're onto something.

If you decide to go to Clapham by tube, don't get out at Clapham Junction. That's actually Battersea, not Clapham, and it confuses lots of visitors. You should use the Northern Line and get out at Clapham Common.

Warmest

Patrick

To: Patrick Knight <patrick.knight@mymail.com>

From: Molly Cooper <molly.cooper@flowermail.com>

Subject: Re: An address in Clapham

Bless you, Patrick, and bless your (secret) contacts at the bank. Please pass on my massive thanks. I'll head out to Clapham just as soon as I can.

I hope 16 Rosewater Terrace is still there.

Molly xx

To: Patrick Knight <patrick.knight@mymail.com>
From: Molly Cooper <molly.cooper@flower-mail.com>
Subject: Re: An address in Clapham—another long e-mail

I've had the most unbelievably momentous day. A true Red Letter Day that I'll remember for the rest of my life.

Until today all I've ever known about my father was what my grandmother told me— that he was charming and handsome and he swept my mother off her feet, and that he didn't have a lot of money, but managed to make my mum very happy.

Oh, and she would also tell me how excited he was when I was born. How he walked the floor with me when I had colic and was so patient, etc.

I was quite content with these pictures, and because I never knew my parents I didn't really grieve for them. I had Gran, and she was warm and loving and doted on me, so I was fine.

But ever since I've been in London I've been thinking rather a lot about Charlie Cooper. I'd look at things like Nelson's Column or Marble Arch, or even just an ordinary shop window, and I'd wonder if my dad had ever stood there, looking at the exact same thing. I'd feel as if he was there with me, as if he was glad that I was seeing his home town.

The feeling was even stronger today when I arrived in Clapham. Every lamppost and shopfront felt significant. I found myself asking if the schoolboy Charlie had passed here on his way to school. Did he stop *here* to buy marbles or *there* to buy cream buns?

And then I found Rosewater Terrace and my heart started to pound madly.

It's a long narrow street, and it feels rather crowded in between rows of tall brick houses with tiled roofs and chimney pots, and there are cars parked along both sides of the street, adding to the crowded-in feeling. There are no front yards or gardens. Everyone's front door opens straight onto the footpath.

When I reached number 16 I felt very strange, as if tiny spiders were crawling inside me. I stood there on the footpath, staring at the house, at windows with sparkling glass and neat white frames, and at the panels on the front door, painted very tastefully in white and two shades of grey.

The doorknob was bright and shiny and very new, and there were fresh white lace curtains in the window and a lovely blue jug filled with pink and white lilies.

It was very inviting, and I longed to take a peek inside. I wondered what would happen if knocked on the door. If someone answered, could I tell them that my father and his family used to live there? How would they react?

I was still standing there dithering, trying to decide what to do, when the door of the next house opened and a little old lady, wearing an apron and carrying a watering can, came shuffling out in her slippers.

'I was just watering my pot plants and I saw you standing there,' she said. 'Are you lost, dearie?'

She looked about a hundred years old, but she was so sweet and concerned I found myself telling her exactly why I was there. As soon as I said the words 'Charles Cooper', her eyes almost popped out of her head and her mouth dropped like a trap door. I thought I'd given her a heart attack.

It seemed to take ages before she got her breath back. 'So you're Charlie's little Australian daughter,' she said. 'Well, I never. Oh, my dear, of course. You look just like him.'

Daisy—that's her name, Daisy Groves— hugged me then, and invited me inside her house, and we had the loveliest nostalgic morning. She told me that she'd lived in Rosewater Terrace ever since she was married, almost sixty years ago, and she'd known my dad from the day he was born. Apparently he was born three days before her daughter Valerie and in the same hospital.

'Charlie and Valerie were always such great friends,' Daisy told me. 'All through their school years. Actually, I always thought—'

She didn't finish that sentence, just looked away with a wistful smile, but I'm guessing from the way she spoke that she'd had matchmaking dreams for my dad and Valerie. Except Charlie was one for adventure, and as soon as he'd saved enough he set off travelling around the world. Then he met my mum in Australia. End of story. Valerie married an electrician and now lives in Peterborough.

Daisy also told me that number 16 has exactly the same layout as her house, so she let me have a good look around her place, and I saw a little bedroom at the top with a sloping ceiling. My dad's bedroom was exactly the same.

But there are no Coopers left in Rosewater Terrace. At least three families have lived in number 16 since my grandparents died and the house has been 'done up' inside several times.

The best thing was that Daisy showed me photos of Charlie when he was a boy. Admittedly they were mainly photos of Valerie, with Charlie in the background, sometimes pulling silly faces, or sticking up his fingers behind Valerie's head to give her rabbit's ears.

But I felt so connected, Patrick, and I felt as if there'd been a reason I'd always wanted to come to London and now I no longer have such a big blank question mark inside me when I think about my father. In fact, I feel happy and content in a whole new way. That's a totally unexpected bonus.

So thank you, Patrick. Thank you a thousand times.

Oh, and I have to tell you the last thing Daisy said to me when I was leaving.

'Your father was a naughty little boy, but he grew up to be such a charming gentleman.' And she pressed her closed fist over her heart and sighed the way my friends sigh over George Clooney.

I floated on happiness all the way back to the Tube station.

Molly xx

To: Patrick Knight <patrick.knight@mymail. com>
From: Molly Cooper <molly.cooper@flower-mail.com>
Subject: Re: An address in Clapham

Patrick, it's only just hit me—as I pressed 'send' on that last e-mail to you I had the most awfully revealing, jaw-dropping, lightbulb moment.

I'm in shock.

Because now when I think about my dreams of dating a perfect English gentleman, I have to ask if it's really some kind of deeply subconscious Freudian search for my father.

I felt quite *eeeeuuuwwww* when I tried to answer that. But where does my interest in gentlemen come from? I mean, it's pretty weird. Most girls are interested in dangerous bad boys.

And this leads to another question. Has becoming acquainted with so much about my father totally cured me of my desire for that impossible, unreachable dating dream? Can I strike the English gentleman off my wish list of 'Things to Do in London'?

I'm not sure. Right now I'm confused. It's something I'm going to have to think about. Or sleep on.

Molly, feeling muddled...

x

To: Molly Cooper <molly.cooper@flowermail. com>
From: Patrick Knight <patrick.knight@mymail. com>
Subject: Re: An address in Clapham

What fantastic news about your father!

I'm so pleased we found the right address and that you've had such a good result. Charles Torrington Cooper sounds as if he was a great guy (a gentleman, no less). Lucky you, Molly. Cherish that image.

I say that selfishly, perhaps, because my own father has caused me huge disappointment and I haven't forgiven him. It's not a nice place to be.

Don't get too hung up on trying to psychoanalyse yourself or your dating goals, Molly. I doubt we can ever understand how our attraction to the opposite sex works. And why would we want to? Wouldn't that take all the fun out of it?

Besides, you've only been in love with the idea of your perfect Englishman. Until you try the real thing you won't be able to test your true feelings.

Molly, you seem to me to be a woman with high ideals and fine instincts. Forget my warnings. I was being overly protective.

Take London by storm and have fun.

Patrick

To: Patrick Knight <patrick.knight@mymail. com>
From: Molly Cooper <molly.cooper@flower-mail.com>
Subject: Surrender

Thanks for your kind and very supportive words, but I'm afraid they came almost too late. I've caved, Patrick. In one fell swoop I've wiped two of my goals from the board.

Rule 1: Avoid other Aussies.
Rule 3: Fall in love with an Englishman.

I've been out with an Aussie guy.

I know what I said about not mixing with Australians, but I realise now that I was limiting myself needlessly. It makes sense that I'd get along better with a fellow countryman.

And besides, Brad's kinda cute—a really tall, sunburned Outback Aussie, a sheep farmer from New South Wales.

Brad may not take me to Ascot or to Covent Garden, but who did I think I was anyway—Eliza Doolittle?

When he came into the Empty Bottle the other night it was like something out of a movie. Heads turned to watch him, and he strode straight up to me at the bar with a big broad grin on his suntanned face.

'G'day,' he said, in a lazy Australian drawl and I have to say our accent had never sounded nicer. 'I remember you,' he said. 'You were on my plane coming over from Sydney. We said hi. Don't you remember?'

I hadn't remembered him (don't know why, because he's very attractive), but I mumbled something positive and I smiled.

'I sat on the other side of the aisle,' he said. 'I wanted to catch up with you when we landed, but I lost you in the crowds at Heathrow.'

Can you see why a girl might find that flattering, Patrick? We were on a plane together more than a month ago, and yet Brad recognised me as soon as he walked into a crowded London bar.

He doesn't want to sit around talking about

home, and that's another reason to like him. He worked as crew on a yacht from Port Hamble to Cascais in Portugal, and then he crewed on a fishing boat back to England. You have to admire his sense of adventure.

I told him about the book of London's secrets that you sent me, and tomorrow we're going to go to Highgate Hill to find Dick Whittington's stone. I used to love the story about Dick and his cat, and the bells that made him turn around. Did you know that Dick really was Lord Mayor of London (four times), and that he gave money to St Thomas's hospital as a refuge for unmarried mothers? That's pretty amazing for way back in the 1300s.

So at least Rule 2—educate myself about the 'real' London—remains intact.

Don't feel sorry for me, Patrick. I'm happy. Brad's a nice bloke, and he seems pretty keen on me, so he's helped me to get over the whole silly idea of a dream date with an English gentleman.

I bet you're highly relieved that you've heard the last about that!

Best

Molly

CHAPTER SIX

To: Felicity Knight: <flissK@mymail.com>
From: Patrick Knight: <patrick.knight@my-mail.com>
Subject: I'll be there to dance at your wedding.

Hi Mother

This is a quick note to let you know that I'm definitely flying over for the Big Day.

This morning I jumped straight onto the internet and made the bookings, so everything's all sorted and I'm really looking forward to seeing you both. I can't believe that I almost allowed this blasted writing project to get in the way of something so significant.

Nothing's as important as seeing you and Jonathan tie the knot.

I'll be there with bells on (or in this case in white tie and penguin suit).

Much love
Patrick

To: Molly Cooper <molly.cooper@flower-mail.com>
From: Patrick Knight <patrick.knight@mymail.com>
Subject: Re: Surrender

Dear Molly

It appears that you're pleased with the latest turn of events in Chelsea (i.e. your New South Wales sheep farmer), so I suppose your change of heart must be a good thing. But I can't help thinking it's a damn shame that none of my fellow countrymen have stepped up to the mark.

However, I do understand the appeal of someone from home when you're so far away, and I suppose there's no harm in breaking your own rules. If the rules have become outmoded they're not much use to you, are they?

From your e-mail, it sounds as if your new Australian escort is more than acceptable to you, and it sounds as if he's also very keen on you, so of course you must be flattered.

Just the same, I feel compelled to repeat the same advice I gave you once before—take care.

Regards
Patrick

Private Writing Journal, Magnetic Island, May 13th

Take care?

Did I really say that? Again?

If only there was a way to retract e-mails. How could I have told Molly to take care with her new Australian boyfriend? What an idiot.

It's not as if she's a helpless child. She's a grown woman—only four years younger than I. And she's on familiar ground now. She's dating the kind of fellow she's no doubt dated many, many times.

Who on earth do I think I am? Her big brother? Her priest?

OK, maybe she's all alone in the world, and in a completely new environment, but that doesn't mean I should try to stand in for her family. I have no inclination to be her father figure.

What's my excuse? Why am I so over-protective? And why did I try to warn her off this Brad character? It's crazy, but I find myself wishing he'd jump on another yacht and take off around Cape Horn, or go climb the North Pole—anything that would take him far away from Molly.

Anyone would think I was jealous of him,

but that's impossible. I don't even know Molly. I've never met her and I have no plans to meet her.

Unless e-mails count.

I suppose e-mails are a form of meeting. They're certainly a very clear form of communication, and all over the globe friendships and relationships are forged via the World Wide Web. But it's not as if Molly and I are cyber-dating.

And yet, when I think about it, we are in rather unusual circumstances. We're exchanging very regular e-mails, and we're living in each other's houses. And if I'm honest I must admit that I do feel as if I know Molly incredibly well, even though we've never really met. In many ways I actually know more about her than I've known about the women I've dated.

I know her hopes and dreams and her fears, and to my surprise I find myself caring about them. I've even had my mother and colleagues from work involved in helping her. I can't ever recall doing anything like that for a girlfriend.

Each day I look out of the windows of Molly's cottage, at the view that has been her view for her whole life, and I think of her. I think of her when I switch on her kettle and use her coffee cups, when I boil an egg in her saucepan and use one of her crazy purple and pink striped egg cups. I even think of her when I drag out her damn vacuum cleaner and give the floors a once over.

Worse, I find myself leaping out of bed in the mornings (out of Molly's bed, as she likes to remind me) and racing to switch on the laptop, hoping that a message might have come from her during the night.

During the day, when I'm supposed to be writing, I find myself waiting to see the little envelope pop up in the bottom right-hand corner of my screen, telling me that I've got a message (as if she'd be writing to me in the middle of the UK night).

I've let myself become incredibly involved with her, and it's like she's become part of my life. I even find myself wishing she was here, wandering about this cottage in her bikini and a sarong.

Actually…there are a couple of beautiful isolated bays where locals tell me you can skinny-dip without being hassled. Now, that's an arresting thought…Molly, slipping starkers into the crystal-clear waters of Rocky Bay.

I've gone barking mad, haven't I? It must

be this solitary lifestyle that's messing with my head.

Clearly I need to get out of this house.

Well, I'll achieve that when I go back to the UK for the wedding. A weekend of mixing with my family and some of my old crowd will soon clear my head.

Already, just the thought of seeing them makes me feel saner. And now I'm asking myself why I was so worried about writing two words in an e-mail. It's not as if Molly will take any notice of my 'take care' warning. She'll have the good sense to laugh at it.

To: Patrick Knight <patrick.knight@mymail.com>
From: Molly Cooper <molly.cooper@flowermail.com>
Subject: Having a good time
Hi Patrick
Unfortunately I can only fit in sightseeing jaunts around my work schedule, but Brad and I have still been getting around. Yesterday we investigated Cleopatra's Needle, which was rather impressive. It's hard to believe it's over three and a half thousand years old and was lying in the desert sands of Egypt until some

English fellow dragged it back to London behind a steamer.

While I was at work Brad went off on his own to check out the Cabinet War Rooms Museum. They're leftovers from WW2, and still hidden away in tunnels and offices beneath Whitehall. Brad's interested because his grandad served over here as a fighter pilot, but I was quite pleased to miss that trip. I'm still a bit iffy about spending too much time underground.

All's well here. Hope you're fine, too.

Molly

To: Molly Cooper <molly.cooper@flowermail.com>
From: Patrick Knight <patrick.knight@mymail.com>
Subject: Re: Having a good time

Molly, I'm glad you're having such a fine time, and I'm pleased to report that I've made some exciting discoveries of my own. You're not the only one who can break rules, you know. I've taken entire days away from the laptop to go skin-diving. Now that the stinger season is well and truly over I feel as if I need to make up for lost time, so I bought myself a snorkel, goggles and flippers and headed down to Florence Bay.

Every day this week I've spent hours and hours in the sea. I'm surprised I haven't grown gills.

I'm hooked. It's amazing. Mere metres below the surface, I enter a different and fascinating world. The water is a perfect temperature, the visibility is excellent, and as you know it's like swimming in a huge aquarium, surrounded by millions of colourful fish.

Thanks to your fabulously helpful illustrations, I've been able to identify lionfish, trigger fish, blue spotted stingrays, clownfish—and of course our cheeky friend Chelmon rostratus.

I was so excited when I saw him poking his long stripy snout out from a piece of pink coral! I almost rang you just to tell you. I suppose I felt a bit the way you did the first time you spotted a film star on the King's Road.

Honestly, I've dived in the Mediterranean and the Red Sea, and I thought those reefs were beautiful, but I hadn't dreamed the reefs on this island would have so much diversity.

Using your map as my guide, I've now dived in all the main bays—Radical, Alma, Nelly, Geoffrey—and I've loved them all. Especially the range of corals in Geoffrey Bay.

The locals tell me that these are only fringing reefs. If I really want to see something spectacular I should head out to the main Great Barrier Reef. So, as you can imagine, that's on the agenda now as well.

I think I'll catch one of the big catamarans when they're passing through on their way to the reef. I can't wait. I might even head north to stay on one of the other Barrier Reef islands for a while.

Sorry, if I'm sounding carried away, Molly. I think I am.

Regards
Patrick

To: Patrick Knight <patrick.knight@mymail.com>
From: Molly Cooper <molly.cooper@flower-mail.com>
Subject: Re: Having a good time

It seems we're both reaping the rewards of our daring decisions to break our own rules. I'm so pleased you're enjoying the island's reefs, Patrick. I got quite homesick reading your descriptions, and I found myself wishing I was there with you, sharing the excitement of your discoveries. Shows how greedy I am, because I wouldn't want to miss all the fun I'm having here.

Yes, I know I can't have my cake and eat it, too.

But, still...skin-diving with you would be so cool.

I hope you enjoy your trip to the Great Barrier Reef, or to other islands further north. Don't go if the weather's rough, though. I'd hate you to be horribly seasick.

Cheers!
Molly

To: Patrick Knight <patrick.knight@mymail.com>
From: Molly Cooper <molly.cooper@flowermail.com>
Subject: Quiet

You've been very quiet, Patrick, so I'm assuming you must have gone out to the Great Barrier Reef, or perhaps you're exploring further afield. Please don't tell me you've found another island you like more than Magnetic.

Molly

Private Writing Journal, Lodon, May 23rd
I almost didn't bring this journal back to London, but I threw it in my bag at the last minute because writing in it has become

something of a habit. My thoughts (sometimes) become clearer when I put them on paper. So here I am, two days after my mother's wedding, pleased and relieved that it was the beautiful, emotional and happy event that both she and Jonathan wanted and deserved.

My duty phone call to my father in Scotland is behind me, so now I'm considering my options.

To see or not to see Molly.

To fly straight back to the island, or stay on here in London for a bit.

The thing is, I'm desperate to call on Molly while I'm here. I'll admit I'm utterly fascinated by her (and my mother could hardly stop talking about her), but I'm hesitating for a number of reasons.

1. The Australian boyfriend. It probably sounds churlish, but I don't think I could enjoy Molly's company if Brad the sheep farmer was hanging around in the wings.

2. Our house swapping agreement. I've handed over my house for three months in good faith, and if I suddenly turn up on Molly's doorstep in the middle of that time she'll be placed in a confusing situation—not sure if she's my hostess or my house guest. I guess this hurdle is one we could work our way around, but then there's—

3. The fantasy date with a gentleman. Here's the thing: I have the right accent and the right clothes to meet Molly's criteria, and if I was on my best behaviour I could probably pull off the role of an English gentleman. I could even take Molly on her dream date to the theatre. In fact, I'd love to.

But—

Maddeningly, I have a string of doubts...

• Does she still want that 'dream' date now that she has her Australian?

• Just how perfect does this Englishman have to be? A movie star I am not.

• What if I try to do the right thing by her, but she misinterprets my motives? Might she think I'm amusing myself at her expense? After all, she's spilled out her heart to me. She might feel horribly embarrassed if I turned up and tried to act out her fantasy.

So where does that leave me? I suppose I could arrange to meet her on neutral ground—in a little café somewhere. Or perhaps I should just phone her for a chat. But then I wouldn't see her, would I?

To: Patrick Knight <patrick.knight@mymail.com>

From: Molly Cooper <molly.cooper@flower-mail.com>

Subject: You're never going to believe this, Patrick!

I don't know whether you're home from the reef yet, but I'm writing this at midnight because I just have to tell you. The most astonishing, amazing, incredible, miraculous thing.

He... Him... The man of my dreams has turned up on my doorstep.

The most gorgeous Englishman. In. The. World.

I hyperventilate just thinking about him, but I've got to calm down so I can tell you my news.

Patrick, I've met your colleague—Peter Kingston, who, as you know, has been working in South America for the same banking company you work for. Now he's back in London for a short break.

OK, I know you must be asking how I can gush about a new man when I'm supposed to be going out with Brad. No doubt you're thinking I'm the shallowest and ficklest woman in the entire universe.

First, let me explain that Brad left last Friday, heading off on another adventure, with no definite plans to come back this way. He's now somewhere at the top of Norway in the Arctic Circle, looking for the Midnight Sun.

He wanted me to go with him, but, while I'm sure the sun at midnight is well worth seeing, I didn't want to spend my hard-earned cash chasing off to another country when there's still so much of England that I haven't seen.

As you mentioned once in an e-mail, the rural parts of England are beautiful. I can't leave without seeing at least some parts beyond London, so other countries will have to come later.

Besides, Brad was fun to go out with here in London, but he was never the kind of guy I'd follow to the ends of the earth.

So, Brad had gone, and it was a Monday night—one of my nights off—and I was having a quiet night in. Oh, you have no idea, Patrick. I was at my dreckest, with no make-up and in old jeans, an ancient sweater and slippers (slippers—can you imagine anything more octogenarian?).

Worse, I was eating my dinner on my lap in front of the telly, and when the front doorbell rang I got such a surprise I spilled spaghetti Bolognese all down my front.

I was mopping bright red sauce from my pale grey sweater as I headed for the door, and then I was stuffing tissues into my back pocket as I opened the door. And then, as they say all the time on American TV—Oh. My. God.

Patrick, let me give you a female perspective on your work colleague.

He's tall. He's dark. He's handsome. The nice, unselfconscious kind of handsome that goes with chocolate-brown eyes and a heart-stoppingly attractive smile.

And when he spoke—you know where this is going, don't you? Yes, he has a rich baritone voice, and a beautifully refined English accent, and I swear I almost swooned at his feet.

The only thing that stopped me from fainting dead away was my need to make sure he hadn't rung the wrong doorbell by mistake.

There was no mistake, thank heavens. Number 34 was Peter's destination. But, to be honest, our initial meeting was a teensy bit awkward. I was flustered. Of course I was. Can you blame me? And I guess my blushing confusion flustered Peter, too.

He seemed rather nervous and uncertain, and I couldn't help wondering if you'd given him orders to call on me. If you did, were you setting yourself up as a matchmaker?

Anyway... We both tried to talk at once, and then we stopped, and then he smiled again and said, ever so politely, 'You go first, Molly. You were saying...?'

Oh, he was the perfect gentleman. He kept his eyes averted from the sauce stains on my chest while I stumbled through my story of why you weren't here and why I was living in your house. Then he explained who he was.

Once that was sorted, and it was clear after a few more prudent questions that we were both at a bit of a loose end, Peter asked ever so casually if I'd like to go out for a drink. I'm afraid I had to wait for my heart to slide back to its normal place in my chest before I was able to accept his invitation.

In no time Peter was comfortably settled on your sofa and watching TV, while I scurried upstairs to change.

If there was ever a wardrobe crisis moment when a girl might wish for a fairy godmother, that was it. The jeans and T-shirts I'd worn on dates with Brad were totally unsuitable to wear out for a drink with Peter. He was in a suit! (No tie, admittedly, but still, a suit's a suit.)

I might have found it easier to think about

clothes if my brain hadn't been swirling like a Category 5 cyclone. Here I was, with a chance to go out with my dream Englishman, and I was freaking out. I was very afraid I wasn't up to the challenge.

Panic attack!!

Thank heavens the possibility of failure snapped me out of it. How could I not go out with this man? Till the end of my days I would never forgive myself. And in a strange way I also felt I owed it to you, Patrick. You sounded rather disappointed that I'd given up on my Englishman.

So I fell on my camel suede skirt like an old friend—the same skirt I wore to afternoon tea with your mother—and the gods must have been smiling on me, for I found a clean silk shirt and tights with no ladders.

I can't do fancy make-up, so applying lip-gloss and mascara didn't take long, and there's not a lot a girl can do with my kind of curly hair, so Peter was pleasantly surprised when I was back downstairs inside ten minutes.

He gave me the warmest smile, as if he quite liked how I looked, and off we went. Not to the Empty Bottle, thank heavens. Peter quite understood about avoiding my workplace.

We went to a bar that I hadn't even noticed

before. It's so discreet it just looks like someone's house from the outside. (Another of
London's secrets?) Inside, there were people
gathered in couples or small groups, and everyone was comfortably seated on barstools
or in armchairs, which made a pleasant change
from the noisy Empty Bottle, which is usually
standing room only.

After our awkward start, I was surprised to
feel quite quickly at ease. Sitting there with
Peter in comfortable chairs, sipping my Sloe
gin fizz and gazing into his lovely dark coffee
eyes, I should have been dumbstruck with
awe, but he has the same easy way that your
mother has.

Is that something well-bred people learn?
Are they given lessons in how to put other
people at their ease?

Anyway, I found myself chatting happily. I
don't suppose that surprises you, considering
the way I chat on endlessly with you.

Peter asked what I'd seen of London, and
I told him about some of the things I'd discovered—like the Kensington Roof Gardens
and the tiny old pub in Ely Street—and to my
surprise he was really interested. He said he'd
lived here nearly all his life and hadn't known
about them. I told him about the book you'd

so kindly sent to me, and tomorrow we're going to do some more exploring together.

Me and Peter Kingston. Can you believe it?

Patrick, I've just realised how long this e-mail is. Sorry, I've been carried away. But I'm sure you have the gist of my news, and I suppose I should try to get some beauty sleep. I'll tell you more after tomorrow (or you can tell me to shut up, if it's all a bit much).

Don't worry, Patrick. I won't do anything rash. I have a highly efficient built-in jerk-detector, and I just know deep in my bones that I'm safe with Peter. But I will try to follow your very sweet advice and *take care!*

Yours, bubbling with too much excitement
Molly x

CHAPTER SEVEN

To: Patrick Knight <patrick.knight@mymail.com>
From: Molly Cooper <molly.cooper@flower-mail.com>
Subject: London explorations

Dear Patrick

I hope you're having as fabulous a time on the Great Barrier Reef as I'm having here. I could carry on about the way discovering London with Peter just keeps getting better and better, so that each discovery is more interesting and fascinating than the last. But you'll be relieved to hear that I'm going to save you from that kind of bombardment and give you a brief overview only.

I saw my last message to you on the screen and almost had a fit. Sorry I rambled on so much, but meeting Peter was all so unexpected and so exciting.

However, I would like to tell you about

our excursion to Westminster Bridge. Now, I know it's not exactly a secret or hidden part of London, but have you ever seen the movie *A Westminster Affair*? It's one of the few movies I saw on the big screen when I was very young, and that day has always been a standout memory for me.

My gran and I caught the ferry over to Townsville on the mainland and we went to the big cinema complex. I can remember every detail, like eating the hugest choc-topped ice creams while we waited for the show to start, and then the movie was just the most beautiful sappy romance. (I won't bore you with the details.)

Afterwards we were both a bit weepy when we came out blinking in the late-afternoon light. Then, to cap things off, we went to a Chinese restaurant and ate big bowls of wonderful chicken soup with floating wontons.

Finally we caught the ferry home, and Gran and I sat out the back, watching the mainland slip away while a cool breeze blew in our faces, and we smelled the sea, and we watched the most gorgeous sunset colour the sky and the water. I've always thought of that day as one of the most perfect days of my life.

Which is probably why *A Westminster Affair*

has remained my all-time favourite film, and you'll understand why it was incredibly special for me to be there on the bridge with a man like Peter.

We admired the magnificent Coade stone lion that guards one end of the bridge. (Did you know a woman invented the special cement that stone is made from?) And we walked across the Thames, and it was a beautiful morning, and it was just like those lines from Wordsworth's poem.

Ships, towers, domes, theatres, and temples lie
Open unto the fields, and to the sky;
All bright and glittering in the smokeless air.

Sorry if that looks like I'm showing off. I'm not really a poetry buff, but because of my soft spot for Westminster I looked up the poem years ago.

Peter and I didn't just walk on the bridge, though. We climbed Big Ben's clock tower. That was Peter's suggestion. I had no idea you could go up there.

'My father brought me here when I was five

years old,' he told me as we started up the three hundred and thirty-four stairs.

It was rather fun, climbing all those stairs together, going past the cell where the famous suffragette Emily Pankhurst was held for some time, poor thing.

We walked behind the illuminated clock faces of Big Ben, and heard the tick-tick-ticking in the clock room.

As we watched the busy cogs and wheels, Peter told me that his father had made him stand in front of this machinery while he gave him a lecture about time marching on.

'He told me that this was my life ticking away,' Peter said. 'And that none of us knows how much time we've been allotted. Time's precious and we mustn't waste it.'

'That's rather a grim message for a little boy,' I suggested.

Peter smiled a little sadly. 'I guess it was. Considering I no longer respect the man, it's surprising that the message stuck.'

I didn't like to ask why he no longer respected his father. Instead I said, 'Does that mean you don't ever waste time?'

'I try not to.'

He reminded me of you, Patrick, and the way you've worked so hard at the bank and how you're still working hard when you're supposed to be on holiday. At least you were until recently. I'm glad you're taking a break now, on the Great Barrier Reef.

I told Peter that maybe he should try living on a tropical island.

One of his eyebrows shot up. 'Does time stand still on your island?'

'It can if you let it,' I said.

He smiled again, rather ambiguously, I thought. Then we went to the belfry and waited while the hammers struck the famous big bells.

Wow.

As you can imagine, there's a great booming sound. But it's not deafening, which was a relief. Just the same, the resonance penetrated all the way through me—rather like the way Peter's smile vibrates through me.

It was a very moving experience, actually, and Peter's eyes were extra shiny. As the gong faded he stared at me for ages, and then he reached for my hands and drew me closer and I knew he was going to kiss me.

My heart started booming louder than Big Ben. How utterly romantic to be kissed by my gorgeous Englishman high above the Thames and the London Eye and the thousands of rooftops and spires.

We shared a beat or two of delicious hesitation and then we inched closer. I was in heaven.

But just at the crucial moment a group of noisy tourists burst into the belfry and we lost our opportunity.

The beautiful moment when we might have kissed is now forever gone, which I suppose proves that his father was right about time and opportunity.

Gosh, Patrick, I'm sorry. I've rambled on, after all.

Molly x

The message *Subject: London Explorations* **has not been sent. It has been saved in your drafts folder.**

Molly's Diary, Chelsea, May 25th

I've decided a diary is a necessity right now. I couldn't send that e-mail to poor Patrick. The dear fellow has been very tolerant of my long-winded ramblings, and it's been wonderful to have him to talk to. But there are some things a girl shouldn't share—especially now that I've met one of his friends and I seem to be falling head over heels. That's too much information for any man.

I guess it's just as well that Patrick's away. I hope he's having a fabulous time, partying like mad at some luxurious Barrier Reef resort.

Actually, the person I really should be talking to now is Karli. She's been my best friend since we were born—or at least that's how it feels—but now that she and Jimbo have sold their computer and left for Cairns, she's out of touch.

Boy, is she going to be mad when she realises she's missed this golden opportunity. She's been waiting to discuss my love life since I was ten years old, but apart from one or two teenage crushes, and a couple of semi-serious boyfriends who eventually left the island, there's been nothing very exciting to report until now. We're both so over talking about her and Jimbo.

So…as I can't pour out my innermost feelings to Patrick or to Karli, I've turned to this diary. Which isn't a new phenomenon for me. When really big things happen in my life I've always felt an urge to write them down. I wrote scads when I was a teenager—espe-

cially when I first started at high school on the mainland and felt so lonely.

Then last year, after Gran died, I wrote in my diary for weeks and weeks. It was as if I needed to get every sweet memory of her down on paper—the exact shape of her smile, her gentle hands and the blue sparkle in her eyes.

I wrote about all the feelings locked inside me, too. How I felt about losing her and why I loved her and how much I owed her, and how I knew she regretted that I hadn't gone to university. It was indeed a pity that I didn't get to extend the wonderful education she scrimped and saved to give me, but how could I have left her when she was so ill and doddery for the last few years? She needed me.

I cried oceans while I wrote, but in a weird way I think the writing helped to ease the painful knots of grief inside me. Eventually I was able to let some of it go.

So now that I've met someone as amazing as Peter Kingston, I have to get stuff down on paper or I'll simply explode.

But where do I start? With his dashing dark looks? His gorgeous smile? His sexy, sexy voice? It's just so amazing that this man is the incarnation of everything I ever dreamed of—good-looking and charming, with a divinely refined English accent that sends delicious shivers all the way through me. And on top of all of these assets he's just absolutely nice.

And he has perfect manners. In fact he's so perfectly lovely I could eat him.

I keep wondering if I've done something very good in a past life. Or perhaps the stars are perfectly aligned in my personal cosmos? Surely some special form of magic brought Peter to my doorstep?

I know I've never felt remotely like this before. This is so much more than a crush. It's like I'm so constantly high I'm practically flying.

Should I be frightened? Might I fall?

I keep telling myself to calm down. I know Peter's only in London for a week, and I know he's only amusing himself in my company while he's here, and I know that he'll soon be back in South America. But he's persuaded me to ask for a few days off work from the Empty Bottle so that we can do lots together, and to my surprise they said yes—no problem.

And he does seem to be having a really good time. With me!

So for the moment I'm going with the flow (which feels a bit like a flash flood)—and I'm reminding myself every so often to breathe.

I haven't even mentioned my biggest piece of news yet.

This afternoon, after an expedition to elegant Hampstead and its many gorgeous, gorgeous houses, Peter and I were walking back from Sloane Square when he reached into his coat pocket and ever so casually produced two tickets.

'My cousin plays cello in the orchestra at the Royal Opera House and she gave me these,' he said, with his lovely, twinkling, careful smile. 'I've no idea if ballet's your cup of tea, but I wondered if you'd like to give it a try.'

I confess I squealed. I know, I know—I should have been more composed and ladylike. Thank heavens I didn't also give in to my impulse to leap on poor Peter and hug him to death.

But it just seemed too much to have the last part of my dream fall into place—an invitation from a lovely Englishman to an evening of culture. Better still, I've been invited to something that's both cultured and *romantic.*

The ballet is Romeo and Juliet *and I know that story inside out. I can recite whole sections of Shakespeare's balcony scene. I adore it.*

After I'd accepted (breathlessly, but politely, I hope) Peter told me that there's a restaurant at the Opera House and he suggested we should dine there, as well. We could have a starter and a main course before the show and then dessert at interval.

Be still my beating heart!

Eliza Doolittle, stand aside.

And I've made what is, for me, a hugely rash decision. I've been so cautious about spending money, but my bank balance is actually healthier than I expected, so I've decided that I can afford to pinch a portion of my savings to buy a new outfit (I really don't think my faithful camel suede skirt is quite right for dinner and the ballet at the Royal Opera House, Covent Garden).

I can afford a new dress. Maybe even a nice piece of jewellery to set it off. I've set tomorrow aside for shopping. Squee!

Maybe I should buy a lottery ticket before my good luck runs out.

To: Patrick Knight <patrick.knight@mymail.com>

From: Molly Cooper <molly.cooper@flower-mail.com>

Subject: How are you?

Hi Patrick

I assume you're still exploring the wonders of the reef? I hope you're having a great time. All is going very well here.

Molly

Private Writing Journal, May 26th

I hesitate to admit on paper that I'm pretending to be someone I'm not. I've never thought of myself as an actor, but I must admit it's fun to take on a role. It all happened so spontaneously—as soon as I saw Molly. I suddenly wanted to become someone better than myself. The man she'd invented in her imagination.

As soon as she told me that Brad the Australian was no longer on the scene, I suppressed my impulse to cheer and instead interpreted his absence as a very clear green light.

So now Molly and I are having a great time. Molly's fabulous, so lively and engaging, and she's so incredibly excited about our planned date. I refuse to spoil this fun by worrying about when or if I should tell her the truth. For once in my life I'm having fantastic, incautious fun, and everything about this planned venture feels right.

Nothing ventured, nothing gained, etc.

Molly's Diary, May 27th

I know I have turned a corner tonight.

I've had the most wonderfully romantic and incredibly special evening, and I feel as if I'm a different person in some mysterious but vitally important way. (I'm wondering if I'm a late bloomer and I've finally grown up.)

I'm sure I can't still be the same overly excited twenty-four-year-old who wrote that rave in yesterday's diary entry. I feel calmer, safer, happier, surer.

Peter kissed me tonight, and I know I'll never be the same again.

But perhaps I should start at the beginning.

I had the most fabulous time shopping. It was a little overwhelming, of course, after living on the island, where there are just two dress shops both specialising in resortwear. Today I was shopping in London, which has thousands—yes, that's right—thousands of shops filled with dresses!

Instead of my usual experience of finding just one outfit that might do, for the first time in my life I had an endless range of clothes to choose from.

Did the vast array of choices do my head in?

Well, yes, I think I did get high from trying things on. I was like those women in movies who go on shopping sprees and try on scads and scads of dresses—whatever takes their fancy—except I didn't parade my dresses in front of anyone. I didn't even have a friend to consult, which was a pity.

But I'm pleased to report that I did not listen to the salesgirls, every one of whom told me that every single dress looked absolutely fabulous on me.

I took my time and I was careful, even though I wanted to be bold and reckless like Patrick's heroine, Beth Harper. It would have been scary but so exciting to have bought something like Beth's expensive little cocktail dress in show-stopping red. But I have to be so careful with my money, so I decided to play it safe. Even so, I'm happy.

I settled on a simple, sleek black cocktail

dress that makes me feel beautiful and sexy. Honestly.

I love it! It fits me like it was made to measure and it feels so soft and sensuous against my skin. It's a truly feel-good, confidence-boosting dress. I teamed it with a lovely woven gold choker necklace, and I think the whole effect struck exactly the right note for this evening.

I also went to the make-up counter in one of the swishest department stores and had my face 'done'.

'Keep it subtle,' I pleaded, and the girl with brightly dyed hair surprised me by doing exactly that. She made my complexion look almost as soft and fine as an English girl's and she made my eyes look huge! Wow, I had no idea clever make-up could make such a difference. I have a new ambition. I'm determined to learn how to do that kind of make-up for myself—although I don't suppose I'll need it when I'm back home on the island.

(I don't want to think about that now.)

It was cool this evening, so I needed my coat, which meant that Peter didn't see my new dress until we got to the cloakroom. When I took the coat off I have to say the expression on his face was a perfect moment—exactly like something out of one of my favourite movies.

He told me I looked beautiful, and his voice was choked, and his throat rippled. And I almost cried.

I'm so glad I didn't. Think of the make-up disaster! And I would have hated to spoil such a lovely moment.

I'm sure that wearing my lovely, sophisticated black dress helped me to stay calm. No doubt the dress plus the fact that the most gorgeous man in the entire theatre was at my side. Have I mentioned how absolutely incredible Peter looked in his dark tux? And there he was, paying courteous and focused attention to me. Throughout the whole evening, I felt quietly, confidently, bone-deep happy.

Oh, and I loved the ballet. Thank heavens. I'd only ever been to the Christmas concerts put on by Karli's ballet teacher when we were kids, and I was always terribly bored by them.

There was no chance of being bored tonight. Before the show Peter and I ate—sorry—dined in the most elegant restaurant. We had goat's cheese and peppered pear, followed by fillet of bream, and both these courses were accompanied by proper French champagne.

Fortunately, Gran trained me well, and I had the whole business of the cutlery sorted. Mind you, Peter is so well-mannered he wouldn't have turned a hair if I'd used the wrong knife or fork.

Then we went into the theatre which was even bigger and grander and more gilded and sumptuous than I'd imagined. There were chandeliers and velvet seats and thick lush carpet and the flash of real diamonds among the women in the audience.

As Peter guided me to my seat with a warm hand protectively touching (and electrifying) the small of my back, I did notice more than one feminine glance directed his way, but he only seemed interested in me.

I can write that now without feeling a need to squeal. The fact that Peter seems to really like me is a kind of quiet truth that's settled happily inside me, keeping my heart warm and light.

Of course everything about the ballet was fabulous. I was so moved by the stirring music and the brilliant dancing and the dramatic acting. As for the costumes, the scenery,

*and have I mentioned the man sitting beside
me?—I was entranced.*

*At the interval we went back to the restau-
rant and had a sinfully delicious champagne
trifle for dessert. And then we returned for the
second half of* Romeo *and* Juliet *and it was
so emotional.*

*The performance was beautiful, exciting,
heartbreaking, intimate. I was spellbound. It
was totally possible to feel the pain of those
tragic young lovers.*

But I managed not to cry.

*I think I was still under some kind of
spell.*

*Afterwards, I thought we might have met
Peter's cello-playing cousin, but apparently she was triple-booked that evening, or
something. So Peter brought me home, and it
was time to say goodnight on my (Patrick's)
doorstep, and I tried, rather inadequately, to
thank Peter.*

*Then I saw the look in his beautiful dark
eyes. Serious. Tender. Aching. All at the same
time. My heart began a painful thumping.
My skin burned. I knew what he wanted and
I was almost certain it was the same thing I
was willing to happen.*

'Molly,' he whispered in his gorgeous deep voice. 'You know I'm going to have to kiss you.'

Oh, my.

I was trembling, but it wasn't from fear. I was trembling from very real, very hot desire.

I have to say, when it comes to seduction, gentlemen have it all over bad boys. Here was Peter, more or less asking permission to kiss me, and I had to restrain myself from screaming, 'Yes!'

As an aside, I should mention that I've always understood the general rule that a kiss is the litmus test of dating. I know the bottom line of any guy meets girl situation is chemistry. But, call me fussy, I've always wanted something more.

I've had quite a few kisses in my twenty-four years. I've had kisses from nice guys I've liked but who've left me thinking there's something missing. (Brad would be my most recent example.) And I've had kisses from dubious guys I wasn't too sure about that have really turned me on.

But now I realise I've never had the vital elements coincide—a really nice guy that I liked a lot, and a really hot kiss.

Until tonight.

And here's the wonderful thing I discovered as Peter and I performed a slow, lip-locked two-step through the doorway and into the front hall. Peter Kingston doesn't just look and walk and talk like my dream man, and he isn't just a charming and amusing companion, he's my dream lover.

His lips were warm and sexy and persuasive, and he tasted absolutely, perfectly, fabulously right. He smelled so good I wanted to bury my nose in his neck and stay there till the next Ice Age.

Truth is, I did not behave with ladylike decorum. I wound myself closer than a strangler fig clinging to a tree in the rainforest. As for the rest of my response—let's just say my mouth had a mind of its own. And my hands weren't exactly shy.

But I was following his lead.

I don't think either Peter or I expected the fireworks to be quite so volatile, although I suspect that Karli might tell me my interest in gentlemen was always about getting to this point—discovering the bad boy behind the polite, genteel façade.

Right at that moment I would have been quite happy if he'd regressed all the way back to Cave Man.

Now, however, I'm sitting on my bed and recording the fact that Peter did not stay here tonight, even though I know we both wanted him to. I suppose I'm grateful that he remembered he's a gentleman and left before things got out of hand.

I mean, really, one of us had to be sensible. He's going back to South America in a couple of days, and I'm going back to Australia in a few weeks, so it wouldn't be wise for us to get too involved. It would create all kinds of complications.

Just the same…I have to say that Peter's kiss felt like a beginning rather than a farewell. He lingered over saying goodnight so sweetly, and he looked so torn about leaving that I just knew—as if I was tuned in to his thought waves—that the best was not over yet.

'I'll ring you first thing in the morning,' he promised, before he kissed me one last, deliciously sexy time.

It's a nice thought to sleep on.

Please let me wake up remembering my dreams.

Text message from Patrick Knight, May 27th, 11.55 p.m.: *Hi Simon, sorry to disturb you so late at night. Wonder if we could swap cars tomorrow? I'd like to run down to Cornwall and stay overnight. Yr sporty MG so impressive. P.*

Text message from Simon Knight, May 27th, 11.59 p.m.: *No prob. Who's the lucky passenger? Any girl I know?*

Text message from Patrick Knight, May 28th, 12.03 a.m.: *Huge thanks. Trust u to guess. She's special + new + Aussie.*

Molly's Diary, May 28th

OMG. I've pinched myself black and blue to make sure I'm not still dreaming.

It's only early, but Peter has already phoned to ask me if I'd like to drive down to Cornwall with him. He's borrowed a cousin's sports car, and as it's a nice day he's suggested we can drive with the top down if I liked. We could see Somerset and Devon on the way, and stay overnight in a B&B on the Cornish coast.

I said yes, I'd love that. Thank you very much!

I think I sounded calm, but, honestly, Peter probably has no idea how big this is for me. I'm flashing hot and cold. The dream

*date—our night out at the Royal Ballet—
which I saw as the pinnacle of glam, is pea-
nuts compared with having this gorgeous man
drive me down to Cornwall in a sports car
(with the top down), even if the sports car
is borrowed (especially when we're staying
overnight in a B&B).*

*This is a biggie. I've never actually gone
away for a weekend with a man before. Peter
probably assumes that I have.*

*Actually, I'm not sure if Peter and I will
be sleeping in the same room, but after last
night's kiss I can't help thinking there's a
good chance the option might arise, so I'm
seriously wishing I'd spent some of my money
on new underwear (just in case, you know).
Oh, and a new nightdress would have been
nice.*

*It's too late now. I really must dash and
start packing. Somehow I think this weekend
is going to be a huge turning point in my life.
In the right direction!*

CHAPTER EIGHT

Molly's Diary, May 28th

Disaster!

Of the very worst kind.

Instead of my life turning in a good direction, my whole world has come crashing down. Right now I'm wishing I'd never heard of London, that I'd never left my lovely, safe little island.

I'm heartbroken. Inconsolable. I feel foolish and miserable and conned, and my dreams are dust at my feet.

The Girl Who Thought She Could Fly...has fallen. Big-time.

If Shakespeare was still alive he would probably write a play about me. Molly Cooper: a comic tragedy in three acts.

Oh, help. I have to make myself write this down, even though my heart is bleeding and every word is killing me. I need to get every painful detail down accurately, because there just may be a time in the very dim and very distant future when I'll try to read it again, with a clearer head and in a calmer spirit than I'm experiencing right now.

First, let me say that I am not in Cornwall, nor on the way to Cornwall in a sports car, with or without the top down. I'm still in Chelsea.

And I'm alone.

My overnight bag is sitting on the floor beside me, still packed. I may just leave it that way as an eternal monument to my foolishness.

So what has happened?

Ouch. Gulp. Squirm. Here goes…

This morning, after my last diary entry, I packed in a flurry of enormous excitement— a change of clothes, nightdress, toothbrush, etc. I dressed carefully in my new, authentic slim jeans and a white T-shirt, and I added an elegant sage-green scarf (carefully looped and draped) in case it was cool in an open car. I imagined the trailing ends flapping glamorously in the breeze.

For once I was happy about my curly hair. The wind could do its worst and my curls would look much the same as they always did. Tangled.

The doorbell rang just before nine o'clock, and I flew downstairs.

Peter stood on the doorstep, looking mega-hunky in blue jeans and a black T-shirt. He mustn't have shaved this morning, and a hint of dark stubble outlined his jaw, and his hair was a little mussed, but the whole casual effect only made him look sexier than ever.

Behind him, parked at the kerb, was a very sleek and low and shiny and very British dark green sports car. The man and the car created a picture beyond my wildest dreams, and I knew I was going to be putty in Peter's hands.

I greeted him with a goofy, it's-so-fantastic-to-see-you grin. We hugged and exchanged an excited kiss.

At least I was excited. But it was about then that I noticed Peter wasn't grinning. He looked—to my complete surprise—nervous.

'Is everything OK?' I asked, already suspecting that it couldn't be.

When he tried to smile, he didn't quite pull it off.

He said, 'Molly, before we head off today there's something I need to explain.'

I didn't like the sound of that at all. My stomach took a very unpleasant dive.

'Can I come in?' he asked.

'Sure.'

My legs were shaking as I took him through to the lounge room. We sat in separate chairs—at least I sat, but Peter remained standing. At first I thought he was just being a gentleman, waiting for me to sit down, but then I realised he didn't plan to sit.

What was his problem?

My mind was galloping ahead, trying to guess what he could possibly need to tell me. Now. This morning. When we were planning to go away together for a lovely romantic weekend. Why did he look so nervous?

I prayed. Please, please don't let him tell me he has a wife back in Argentina. Or a fiancée. Or even a girlfriend.

I know my expectations of this English gentleman were way over the top, but I couldn't bear to have my lovely man sully his perfect image now.

I wished Patrick hadn't taken off, gallivanting around on the Great Barrier Reef or wherever. If he'd been answering his e-mails he might have warned me...I might have been ready for this.

'Before we head off—' Peter began.

I told myself I was agonising over nothing.

Everything was OK. He was still planning to take me to Cornwall.

'I need to explain exactly who I am,' he said, *giving me a slightly awkward but utterly gorgeous lopsided smile.*

Who I am…?

What on earth could that mean?

In that moment something in his eyes… something about the tilt of his smile… reminded me of someone I'd met recently— since I'd moved to London…

And then in a flash of insight I knew.

It was Felicity Knight.

But how could Peter…?

My skin chilled, and fine hairs rose on the back of my neck a split-second before the truth dawned.

My throat closed over, but I managed to whisper, 'You're not Peter. You're Patrick, aren't you?' Trembling with shock, I fought back tears. 'You're Patrick, pretending to be Peter. Peter doesn't exist. None of this is real.'

CHAPTER NINE

'WHAT happened?' SIMON Knight frowned when he opened his front door and found his cousin on the doorstep. 'Don't tell me—'

His eyes flashed to the kerb.

'It's OK,' Patrick assured him. 'I haven't pranged your car. Not even a scratch.' He forced a weak smile as he held out the keys. 'The trip's off, that's all.'

'That's bad luck.' Simon's sympathy sounded genuine as he pocketed the keys, but his intelligent grey eyes blazed with curiosity. 'So is Cornwall actually off the agenda altogether, or simply postponed?'

'It's definitely off.' Patrick shrugged, hoping the gesture looked casual. 'It's no big deal. I think I'll try to change my flight. Might as well head back to Australia tomorrow.'

Simon gave a sympathetic shake of his head. 'I suppose I'd better fetch your car key. It's in the kitchen.' As he turned to go, he hesitated and looked back at Patrick again with a frown. 'You look like you could use a drink.'

The offer held distinct appeal. Although it was only mid-morning, Patrick had never felt more in need of a stiff drink, and he always enjoyed his cousin's company. They were almost as close as brothers, and without the strain of sibling rivalry. At the wedding Simon had been eager to hear every bit of news about Patrick's stay on the island.

Even so, Patrick was reluctant to offload his disappointment. Simon would never press him for insensitive details about his planned romantic getaway, but it was only reasonable that he would expect their chat to include at least some information about the girl Patrick had planned to take to Cornwall.

Talking about Molly wasn't an option. Patrick was feeling too raw, too devastated, too frustrated and mad with himself. Simon had been telling him for years that he needed to give more time to his women-friends, and to lavish them with his attention. He wasn't about to confess that he'd been willing and ready to do just that with Molly, but instead he'd single-handedly conducted the biggest stuff-up in dating history.

'Thanks, but no thanks,' he told Simon quietly.

'I'll say cheerio for now. I guess I'll see you again at the end of June.'

The men shook hands.

'Well, have a safe trip back. And I hope you have better luck with the rest of the Australian girls,' Simon said with an encouraging wink.

'Sure.'

There was only one Australian girl Patrick wanted to enjoy, and he'd stupidly wrecked his chances with her. It seemed crazy that he was flying back to her house.

Of course he'd phone Molly later, and he'd try again to explain what now seemed totally, ludicrously unexplainable.

The crazy thing was that he'd stuffed up relationships in the past, mainly through selfish neglect, and he'd taken the ensuing rejection on the chin. Female company had only ever been a form of pleasant entertainment. Since when had it become a vital mission?

What was different this time? How had he let one bright-eyed, mouthy Aussie get so deeply under his skin?

Of course he'd never stopped to ask himself why meaningful romance wasn't on his agenda. No doubt a shrink would try to tell him it was all tied up with his parents' messy divorce. He couldn't deny that memories of his mother's distress had upset him deeply, and he'd shied away from marriage and the whole happy-ever-after myth. He couldn't bear to hurt a woman the way his father had.

Was it possible that he'd chosen to meet Molly in disguise so he could avoid facing the uncomfortable truth that he really, *really* liked her?

As Patrick depressed the central locking system for his car he felt hollow and utterly miserable and confused. And completely empty of hope.

Molly's Diary, May 29th

I was too upset to keep writing yesterday. I've spent most of the past twenty-four hours crying, and now my eyes and nose and throat are so sore I feel as if I've been terribly ill.

I've taken the phone off the hook so Patrick can't ring me, and I haven't gone anywhere near my laptop. I don't want to know if he's sent me an e-mail. I'm not ready to talk to him. I don't know if I'll ever be ready.

But I owe it to myself to write down the rest of what happened yesterday. Maybe (vain hope) the act of writing will help somehow.

So...

At first when I guessed the terrible truth and blurted out that Peter was actually Patrick he looked relieved. He smiled and the tension left his shoulders.

Not for long.

Something had snapped inside me. I suppose it was my sense of trust. I'd been lied to. Here I was, on the brink of sleeping with this man in a romantic Cornish B&B, and I'd learned he was a fraud. It was all an act.

As I leapt to my feet, Patrick's smile died.

'What are you doing here?' I demanded. (OK, I might have yelled.) 'You're supposed to be in Australia. Somewhere on the Great Barrier Reef.'

His face seemed to pale, as if my anger really bothered him.

Too bad. He couldn't have been nearly as bothered as I was.

'My mother was married last weekend,' he said. 'It was all rather unexpected and a bit rushed, and I came over for the wedding.'

His mother's wedding? It took me a moment to digest this news. Then I remembered the way Felicity's eyes had shone when she'd talked about her 'friend' Jonathan.

So they were married, and that was nice. Really nice. But what did that have to do with Patrick (or Peter) and me? So what if he'd come home for a family wedding? Why did he have to keep it a secret from me? And how did it give him an excuse to ruin my life?

So many questions were rushing through my head.

'Where have you been staying?'

He shrugged. 'The Lime Tree Hotel.'

Un. Believable.

It was the most ridiculous thing I've ever heard. Why would Patrick Knight stay in a hotel when there were two spare bedrooms here in his *house? I wanted to cry, but I knew I mustn't give in to such weakness. I needed all my strength to deal with this shattering of my dreams. I couldn't bear to think that I'd been part of a game—a source of amusement.*

'How could you?' I shouted, and my voice was as shrill as the proverbial fishwife's. 'How could you go to so much trouble to trick me? How could you be so cruel?'

'I'm sorry, Molly.' Patrick spoke quietly but earnestly. 'I didn't want to hurt you. It seemed like a good plan at the time, but I had no idea—' He raised a hand, as if groping for words, then plunged both hands into his jeans pockets.

'What seemed like a good plan? To totally deceive me?'

'You were so keen to meet your Englishman.'

'Oh, right. I foolishly poured out my heart, and you thought it would be fun to play games with me after your mother's wedding.'

'No. I—' Again, he floundered.

'You felt sorry for me.'

'Well...you sounded so disappointed.'

'You thought I was desperate and you'd lend a hand.'

'I wanted you to be happy.'

'I was happy, thank you. Very happy, as a matter of fact.'

Patrick sighed heavily. His right hand rose again, and this time he ploughed frustrated fingers through his lovely dark hair.

I was frustrated, too. He wasn't making sense. How on earth did he think his deception could have made me happy? It was tearing me apart.

I'd believed in Peter. I'd fallen in love with Peter.

'Why did you have to pretend, Patrick? Why couldn't you have just turned up and said, "Hi, I'm Patrick and I'd like to stay for a few days. And while I'm here why don't we go out?"'

It could have been so perfect, so much fun...

He was so lovely...

Now he'd spoiled everything.

Patrick shook his head. '*I was worried you wouldn't be excited if you knew it was me. It wouldn't feel like a proper romantic date to you. After all those e-mails when you told me so much about your dreams, I was sure that if I simply asked you out you'd think I was just going through the motions because... Well... yes—because I felt sorry for you.*'

'*But you did feel sorry for me!*'

I was so furious I stamped my foot. My eyes filled with tears. Patrick, the man I'd spilled my heart out to...the anchor at the other end of my e-mails...the thoughtful guy who'd warned me to 'take care'...had been pretending, having fun at my expense.

How could he? You idiot, Patrick, I wasn't that desperate.

How could he kill off my lovely, romantic Peter and leave me with...?

Nothing?

He was right about one thing. I didn't want a man who felt sorry for me. But now—

I was forced to accept that the dream man who'd turned up on my doorstep hadn't been surprised to see me at all. And he hadn't suddenly liked what he'd found when I opened the door. Our relationship wasn't spontaneous—not even romantic. He'd been planning it, and he'd arrived determined to ask me out regardless of what I was like.

Our lovely times together were nothing more than a goodwill gesture from a London banker to a poor, hopeless Aussie chick with delusions of grandeur.

I'm pleased to say I was queenly and dignified as I pointed to the door, but I knew that I couldn't hold it together for long. At any minute I was going to break down completely. 'I think you'd better go,' I said.

Patrick looked dismayed, and I think he was about to protest when he realised how serious I was.

He glanced briefly at my overnight bag, packed and ready by the door. 'So you won't—?

'I couldn't possibly go to Cornwall with you,' I said, interrupting him. But I choked back a sob, because although I was very grateful that I hadn't gone away to Cornwall before I found out the truth, I was still bitterly disappointed that I was missing out on so much.

I hadn't just lost my dream man, I'd lost the promise of a lovely weekend.

Which just goes to show how contrary a female can be and still be right!

'Molly, I—'

'Don't say any more, Patrick. Just go, please.'

My old, romantic-movie-watching self might have imagined that Patrick looked stricken—rather like the way Christian looked when he watched Vanessa walk away from him on Westminster Bridge. But then, my old, romantic-movie-watching self had believed in her good radar for detecting jerks.

Huh.

In the fifteen minutes since Peter had become Patrick I'd grown a hundred times older and wiser. And boiling mad to boot.

I opened the door and made a grand sweeping gesture. And, no, I didn't feel awkward about turning Patrick out of his own home. After all, he deserved this, didn't he?

As he moved past me in the doorway, I caught a hint of his special scent. I don't know if that scent is just the way his skin smells naturally, or if it's the cologne he uses. If it is cologne, it's nicer than any male cologne I've ever smelled before. Whatever it is, it's fine-tuned to my senses and fills me with longing.

I sucked in my breath and gripped the door handle to stop myself from leaning in to him.

On the doorstep he turned to me. 'Molly, I'm very sorry I've hurt you. It's the last, the very last thing I wanted.'

Yeah, you and me both, I thought. But I couldn't respond. I was too busy concentrating on not leaning any closer.

'Yoo-hoo, Patrick!' a voice called suddenly.

It was Mrs Blake, Patrick's elderly neighbour, popping her head over the neatly clipped hedge that divided their front gardens.

'Oh, it is you, Patrick,' she gushed. 'I thought I saw you get out of that lovely sports car!'

In the outdoor light I could see that Patrick looked pale and upset, but I steeled my heart.

As always, he was unfailingly polite.

'Good morning, Eleanor.'

Honestly, the neighbour must be at least eighty, but she was ogling Patrick with all the shameless delight of a tweeny fan-girl.

'You're back earlier than we expected.' She

*beamed. 'How absolutely lovely to see you,
my dear. How was Australia?'*

*As if that wasn't bad enough, from across
the street another woman (middle aged and
in a floral dress of pleated chiffon with strings
of pearls) started waving madly.*

'Halloo, there, Patrick,' she called.

*Charming, lovable Patrick Knight. If only
they knew how dangerous this adorable, two-
faced man could be.*

*I shut the door very quickly. OK, yes—I
confess I probably slammed it.*

Molly's Diary, May 31st

*I'm sorry to report that my life is not back
to normal.*

*I was going to try to pretend that every-
thing's fine now, but I can't do it. I've always
hated pretence, and since the Patrick-Peter
debacle I've developed a particular sensitiv-
ity to any whiff of falsehood.*

*So this diary is going to remain brutally
honest. I am still hurt and devastated, and
terribly, terribly angry. So, as you can imagine, I wasn't in the right frame of mind first
thing yesterday morning, when a delivery guy
from a florist's shop tried to deliver armfuls
of roses, carnations, lilies and daffodils.*

Honestly, there were enough flowers to fill every bathtub in the house.

But how could I accept them?

Under any other circumstances (i.e. circumstances that did not involve my faith in men being ripped wide open) I would have been ecstatic, but I told the delivery man he had the wrong address.

He wouldn't believe me. He showed me the address on the docket, and he even offered to ring the store to double-check. So then I had to tell him that I simply couldn't accept the flowers.

I told him I was very sorry, but I was allergic to pollen. I asked him to take them to the hospital, or to give them to his girlfriend or his grandmother, or to anyone he knew who'd appreciate them.

I thought my pollen excuse sounded plausible, but he shrugged and said I wasn't the first young lady who'd refused a delivery of flowers.

'I understand, ducks,' he said as he carried the gorgeous armfuls back to the van. 'Some dimwits never get it through their thick heads that flowers can't make up for each and every sin.'

Too true.

I suppose Patrick expected that these over-the-top and gorgeous flowers would make amends for his deception. Hasn't he any idea how very real my pain is?

If only he knew that over the weekend I've toyed with some terribly wicked ideas for retribution. I've considered:

- *Repainting his bedroom hot pink with black polka dots*
- *Super-gluing his remote control to the top of his TV set*
- *Using a pair of pinking shears to cut out the crotch of the expensive Italian trousers in his wardrobe*
- *Sprinkling chilli powder on his toilet paper roll (just before I leave)*

These were actually the nicer possibilities, but unfortunately they've only given me a momentary glimmer of satisfaction. I suspect that revenge doesn't really suit my personality, because while I was dreaming up these evil schemes one corner of my mind was also busily wishing that there'd been no trickery and I'd gone off to Cornwall.

Duh.

Anyway, after the flowers had gone yesterday (and that was an incident that caused several curtains in Alice Grove to twitch) I decided to get out of the house. I've always preferred to sulk out of doors.

So I went for a long walk along the Chelsea Embankment and all over Battersea Park, trying to shake off my angry mood.

But wouldn't you know it? Everywhere I went there were happy couples. Old, young and every age in between. Jogging together, strolling arm-in-arm, walking his-and-her dogs, pushing babies in prams, sitting on park benches, lying on the grass and gazing into each other's eyes. I swear no matter where I walked I was surrounded by images of blissful, idyllic, dreamy romance!

And of course no matter how hard I tried I couldn't stop my mind from going over and over my own tragic non-romance. So many sweet memories—my first sight of Peter on the doorstep, our London explorations, Westminster and Big Ben, that fabulous night at Covent Garden.

That kiss! Quite possibly the most fabulous kiss in all of history—certainly in all of my history.

I put so much emotional energy into my time with Peter (alias Patrick), and ever since he left I've been fighting useless regrets for what might have/could have/should have happened. How crazy is that? How can I wish for romance with him when I'm mad enough to wring his neck?

The thing is, a part of me can't help wishing he'd never told me the truth on Saturday morning. I was so poised for the thrill of a lifetime—the sports car, the beautiful rural English countryside, the night in a Cornish B&B with my dream man.

If only, if only...

The unrealised romantic potential of that lost weekend in Cornwall haunts me like a tune I can't get out of my head.

And so do all kinds of questions—endless questions that have no answers—questions I wish I'd put to Patrick before I showed him the door.

The biggie that's really bugging me is why he waited until we were leaving for Cornwall to tell me who he was. Why did he wait until after he'd already kissed me?

Come to think of it, why did he ask me to go to Cornwall at all?

He'd already taken me out on the so-called 'dream date'. The deception had been successfully accomplished and his role as my companion was over.

I suppose he'd been planning to exploit

the situation. After our kiss, he knew I was ripe for the plucking. But then his conscience probably got the better of him.

!!!

This anger isn't doing me or my diary any good. I just ripped a blooming great hole in the page with my pen.

I need to calm down. I need to be kind to myself.

I have to remember that I've had a lucky escape and should be celebrating. I should also remember that I was having a great time in London before a certain tall, dark and incredibly handsome man landed on the doorstep, and that I can have a great time again.

I just won't share my future great times with Patrick—the Knight whose armour is no longer shining but severely tarnished and dented.

I shudder when I think of all the things I've told him in my previous e-mails. I just opened my heart and let it all out. He knows so much about me (in particular my penchant for English gentlemen in three-piece suits with lovely plummy voices). I trusted him, and he betrayed that trust.

I think that's what's hurt me most.

The terrible thing is Patrick warned me that an expensive suit and well-bred accent did not turn a man into a gentleman, and I still fell into the trap.

Let's be honest—a true gentleman would never be deceitful.

Even if he was trying to do someone a good turn.

Would he?

Private Writing Journal, June 2nd

I've been back in Australia for three days now, and I still haven't written to Molly. It's more than possible that whatever I say will upset her. The pollen allergy excuse that the florist kindly passed on shows how persona non grata *I am. That's why I've resorted to this journal again. If I'm going to try to make amends, it might be easier to get my thoughts clear on paper before I commit them to e-mail.*

I'm pretty sure it's up to me (as the offender) to make the first move towards reconciliation, and I doubt that either Molly or I will enjoy the rest of our house swap if we continue in uncomfortable silence. But after the way we parted, what can I say to mollify her? (Oh, God, terrible pun.)

Can I offer yet another apology? Try to set things straight? Should I attempt to justify exactly why I started the whole subterfuge fiasco?

Do I actually have a decent excuse for totally stuffing up a perfectly happy girl's life?

It's not the first time I've been accused of doing that, of course, but in the past I've mainly committed sins of omission (e.g. last-minute cancellations of dates). This time I went to the trouble of manufacturing a perfect date, only to have it turn into a perfect disaster.

Molly has every right to ask why. I only wish I knew the right answer, or rather I wish I had an answer that she'd find acceptable.

When I started out on the flight back to the UK my plan was simply to knock on Molly's door and to say hello (yes, as Patrick, not Peter) and to satisfy my curiosity. But as the time to meet Molly drew closer I kept thinking about her big dating dreams. At some hazy point the Peter Kingston scheme emerged, but it wasn't till I saw Molly that I seized on it.

Why?

I suspect I was trying to protect myself. I'd already been entranced by Molly's personality, even though I'd only met her in e-mails, but I was reluctant to get too personally involved. After all, we are house swappers from different worlds, almost different planets. We had no plans for a relationship.

The truth is, I honestly did want that night at Covent Garden to be perfect. Molly had such high expectations of her dream date, and I was sure that she couldn't possibly be happy with a compromise date with a house swapper who'd read all her self-revealing e-mails. I was sure she'd assume I had pegged her as desperate and dateless, that I'd taken pity on her.

So my original motives were chivalrous— or so I thought—but my mistake was to get in deeper, when a ten-year-old could have told me I was asking for trouble.

Of course I should never have kissed her. I should have known that those soft, pink, talkative lips would be my undoing. Of course I should have known that kissing Molly would be beyond amazing and that one kiss could never be enough.

Instead I let the kiss get out of hand (almost), and that led me to an even bigger mistake— the proposed weekend in Cornwall.

How do I explain that one?

I suppose I could claim a longing to share in Molly's enthusiasm for new discoveries, but who's going to believe me? Certainly not Molly. Not after that kiss.

The crazy thing was I trapped myself. I fell for her harder and faster than I would have believed possible. I became the one who was desperate, but I couldn't contemplate sleeping with her without telling her who I really was. I may be casual in my relationships, but I've never been a con man.

And yet telling the truth meant bursting Molly's fantasy bubble.

That was my Waterloo. Thanks to my poor handling of this, our dream date was reduced to a pity date in Molly's eyes. And I was forced to accept that I had fallen for a warm, lovely, real girl, who in turn was in love with a dream.

Molly didn't want reality. How else can I explain her horror at discovering the truth that Peter and I were one and the same?

How could I possibly tell her how I felt when she was looking at me as if I'd murdered someone? (And I suppose I had. I'd murdered her fantasy.)

Now Molly has sent me the strongest possible negative messages—not with words but

*through her actions. She showed me the door.
She refused the flowers. She stopped writing
e-mails.*

*A man doesn't expose himself and declare
his feelings unless he's pretty damn sure he
will be well received, so all things considered
it's pretty clear that continued silence is my
wisest option.*

Molly's Diary, June 6th

*I've kept myself deliberately busy this past
week, especially over the weekend, taking on
as many shifts at the Empty Bottle as they'll
give me. It helps to have something else to
think about besides you-know-who.*

*This morning I'm finally feeling strong
enough (or at least I hope I am) to open my
laptop and take a peek to see if any e-mails
have arrived. I can't help being curious.*

*OK—I've looked. There's only one e-mail
and it's from Karli. Yay! I'm so pleased to
hear from her at last.*

*I think I'm relieved that there's no word from
Patrick. I'm sure he's OK. Of course he is.*

To: Molly Cooper <molly.cooper@flowermail.
com>
From: Karli Henderson <hendo86@flower-
mail.com>

Subject: Back online!!

Hi Molly

Sorry I've taken so long to get back to you. Jimbo and I are at last settled in Cairns, but it's been a mad month, what with packing up and starting new jobs and finding somewhere to live. Yes, I've got a job, too—in the office at the same boatyard where Jimbo works as a shipwright. So we're set, but I haven't had time to scratch myself.

We have a nice flat, and wages coming in, so we're very happy. We bought a second-hand computer (it works most of the time), and we've already made a few new friends. (Although no one will ever replace you as my best friend, Mozza.)

How are you? How's London? Have you found your dream British gentleman? I've been thinking about you so much even though I couldn't write.

Actually, I've just been looking back over our old e-mails (saved on a USB stick), and I've realised that you probably still have no idea what your house swapper looks like. So, honey, I guess it's finally time to satisfy your curiosity. Let me tell you. You might want to come rushing home.

Patrick's tall and dark. (Not a bad start, huh?)

His hair was short when he got here, but it quickly started to grow and curl on the ends. (Very cute.) He has dark chocolate eyes with extra-long lashes. Jodie G verified this when she got a close-up look at him at the party he held after the toad races. But, honestly, I was there, too, and she didn't get as close to him as she likes to make out.

He has a good jawline, and when I saw him there was just the right amount of stubble. (So, yes, your Patrick is smoking hot. Are you drooling yet?) Oh, and he has wide shoulders and a six-pack. (We've seen him walking on the beach with his shirt off.)

So I guess it's no surprise that he's also good at sports. You know how Jimbo always plays in the Bay of Origin rugby league competition? Well, because we were leaving the island, the Sapphire Bay team was one player short. Your Patrick has only played rugby union, not league, but he volunteered to fill in and managed to catch on very quickly.

So, despite our initial concern that he might be a bit aloof, he's turned out to be a great mixer. Actually, he must have been a real bonus to our team, because we won for the first time in about three seasons. Jimbo has his nose out of joint about that. Guys and their tender egos—you've gotta love 'em.

I haven't heard much news since we left. Do write back soon and fill me in with everything that's happened in your exciting world. I miss you heaps!

Lots of love,

Karli x

To: Karli Henderson <hendo86@flowermail. com>

From: Molly Cooper <molly.cooper@flower-mail.com>

Subject: Re: Back online!!

Attachment: Molly's Diary (125KB)

Hi Karli

Thanks so much for your e-mail. You have *no idea* how good it is to hear from you again. I've missed you so much.

There's so much I have to tell you, but first I must say I'm really glad your move to Cairns has worked out so well for you. That's fab. Although I still hate thinking about going back to the island when you won't be there. I'll be so lonely without you.

Thanks also for the info about Patrick, but actually I've seen him now, so I know that your description is extremely accurate. Patrick came back to London for his mother's wedding, you see, and he called in here. Actually, it's a short story, but I've sent you the long version in an attachment to this e-mail.

You'll be mad when I tell you that you were out of reach at a highly crucial point in my life. (My love-life, that is.)

I've used Patrick's scanner and sent you the relevant bits from my e-mails and diary in the attachment. Once you've read everything you'll understand why I needed you.

These pages are for your eyes only, of course. I know I can trust Jimbo, but still, could you please delete them as soon as you've read them?

Oh, and it goes without saying that I need you to write back and tell me what you think. About *everything*. Thanks in advance.

Loads of love to you both

Molly x

To: Molly Cooper <molly.cooper@flowermail.com>
From: Karli Henderson <hendo86@flowermail.com>
Subject: Re: Back online!!

Wow!! I turn my back on you for a few weeks and you turn into a dating diva. Thanks so much for trusting me with your diary pages, Molly. I can't believe Patrick went back to England and actually turned up on your doorstep and took you to Big Ben and Covent Garden and everything.

That. Is. So. Amazing.

I can just imagine how gorgeous you looked in your beautiful new black dress. Can you send me a photo? And how fabulous to see *Romeo and Juliet*. I'd give anything for that. Remember when I was going to be the world's greatest ballerina?

Now, Molly, I know you're upset that Patrick was pretending to be Peter, and as your best friend I totally respect your right to be upset. But, honey, I'm sorry. I don't get it. I really don't understand why you're so angry. Colour me confused, and I apologise in advance, but I don't see what's so wrong with what Patrick did. He gave you your dream date—exactly what you wanted. In my book that's incredibly sweet. I break into a happy dance every time I think about you on that night.

As far as I can tell, reading between the lines, Patrick was rather smitten by how you looked in your sexy black dress, and by your talented kissing, and that's why he wanted to whisk you away to Cornwall. But he didn't

want your relationship to become—ahem—
intimate, unless you knew who he really was.
That's honourable, isn't it?

Clearly I'm not seeing this situation in the
same light as you, Molly. Admittedly I wasn't
there, and I only have your diary to go on.
Sorry if I'm not much help.

Would you like to phone me so we can talk
this over properly?

Love
Karli

Molly's Diary, June 8th

*I'm shocked. I can't believe Karli's not sup-
porting me at the one point in my life when I
need her most. Why doesn't she understand
how I feel?*

*All my life, whenever I've been let down or
disappointed, Karli has been there for me.
She was so understanding and sympathetic
when Gran first got sick and I had to cancel
my plans to go to university.*

*Now she's on a totally different wavelength.
How can she possibly claim that Patrick's
deception was sweet?*

Sweet?

*In a pig's eye. Can't she get how foolish I
felt? How I hated to be strung along? How*

*my trust in Patrick was shaken? Surely it's
painfully obvious that I have every right to
be furious.*

*I think Karli's right about one thing—the
need for a phone call. I'll ring her tomorrow
morning, when it's evening in Australia, and
we'll sort this out. I won't feel right until I
have Karli firmly on my side.*

Molly's Diary, June 9th

*Can't sleep. Am up drinking hot milk
and honey and eating buttered raisin toast.
Comfort food. In the middle of the night. At
least a midnight feast is better than lying in
bed, tossing and turning and trying to work
out what I'm going to say to Karli when I call
her in the morning.*

*Just the same, conversations with her keep
going round and round in my head.*

Karli: Why are you so angry with Patrick?

Me: Because he lied and cheated.

Karli: That's a bit heavy. He was only
trying to make your stay in London perfect.
Admit it, Molly, you were having fabulous
fun with Peter. The time of your life.

Me: Maybe I was, but it was all a sham. It
wasn't real.

Karli: Why did it have to be real?

Me: Because…

Karli: What's that, Molly? I can't hear you.

Me: Because I needed it to be real. It was so wonderful. I fell in love with Patrick when he was pretending to be Peter, and then I lost him. I lost both of them, and I'm devastated because maybe…

Oh, my, gosh…

(Cue evasive mumbling)

Karli: Excuse me, Molly?

Me(whisper): Maybe…I'm still in love with him.

Karli: I'm having trouble with this line. Speak up. I can't hear you.

!!

Help! I think it's true. About still being in love with Patrick, I mean.

Is that the reason I can't stop being angry with him?

I fell totally, crazily, deeply in love with Peter, and I wanted him to be just as totally, crazily, deeply in love with me. But he was only pretending.

My turmoil is actually a mixture of anger and deepest despair. I couldn't bear to know that Patrick was putting on an act. I needed

*him to love me, really love me, but it was all
pretence.*

*And buried beneath my boiling anger is my
deep sense of loss.*

*I think about all those times I spent with
Patrick while he was pretending to be Peter.
If Patrick hadn't been so busy pretending we
could have talked about real things. Things
that mattered to both of us. Our houses,
our friends, his mother, my dad, his novel,
my island, his London. Even the Chelmon
rostratus fish.*

*But, as things were, instead of convers-
ing intelligently with a man who already felt
like a good friend, I spent far too much time
swooning over a fantasy! And now—*

*I don't know! I'm confused. But one thing's
certain—the damage has been done. Deeply
and permanently.*

*And I don't think I'm actually ready to talk
about this with Karli. I thought I wanted to
wallow in a pity party, but now I suspect that
I should just get over myself and move on.*

*I guess the best way to move on is to send
Patrick an e-mail—short and friendly, let
bygones-be-bygones—with not a hint of how
I'm really feeling. I'd hate him to know I'm*

still hurting. I only hope I can strike the right note and sound friendly and interested, but not too interested.

CHAPTER TEN

To: Patrick Knight <patrick.knight@mymail. com>
From: Molly Cooper <molly.cooper@flower-mail.com>
Subject: Safely home?

Dear Patrick

I trust that you had a good flight back to Australia, and that you're now safely on Magnetic Island and all is well—including your writing.

I'm pleased to report that everything is fine here, although Cidalia is in a bit of a flap, which is the main reason for this e-mail. Did you know she's about to become a grandmother at any moment? She's been knitting all kinds of impossibly cute, tiny clothes (even though we're diving into summer here).

If the baby's a boy he will be called Rafael Felipe, and if it's a girl she will be Yasmin Cidalia.

As you can imagine, the telephone at 34 Alice Grove has become a very important instrument. Every time it rings we rush to its summons, hearts a-clanging.

By the way, I didn't mention your recent return to London to Cidalia, and she hasn't said anything to me, so I'm assuming she doesn't know you were here and that it's best to leave it that way.

Best wishes
Molly

Molly's Diary, June 10th

I hope I got the tone of that e-mail right. The last thing I want is to sound like I'm stalking Patrick. I almost reverted to type and carried on about how I love the name Rafael, and how I think Yasmin is beautiful for a baby girl, and how I'm really hoping I get to see the baby. As always, I felt an urge to tell Patrick everything, but I reined myself in, thank heavens.

Now it's time to climb out of my post-Peter/ Patrick depression and get on with my exciting, adventurous and uplifting life in London. (Notice I left out romantic?) I think I've finally bitten the reality bullet. Hip, hip hooray.

To: Molly Cooper <molly.cooper@flower-mail.com>
From: Patrick Knight <patrick.knight@mymail.com>
Subject: Re: Safely home?

Hi Molly

Thanks for your e-mail and, yes, I'm safely back on the island and ensconced once more in Pandanus Cottage.

Thanks for your news about the imminent arrival of Cidalia's grandchild. I'm afraid I've rarely had time to chat with her, and I didn't even know her daughter was expecting—although I do remember a lot of fuss and excitement over her wedding a couple of years ago.

I look forward to hearing news of the safe arrival of little Rafael or Yasmin.

I'm pleased to report that I do have good news about my writing. To my immense relief, it's finally taken off. I've had fresh inspiration, you see, and suddenly I have so many ideas clamouring to be written down that I can hardly type quickly enough. It's rather annoying that I wasted all those weeks when I first arrived here going down the wrong track, but I suppose it's never too late to start again.

If my communication seems minimal during

the rest of my stay here it will be because I'm busily writing this book. At last.

Cheers
Patrick

To: Karli Henderson <hendo86@flowermail. com>
From: Molly Cooper <molly.cooper@flower-mail.com>
Subject: Re: Back online!!

Hi Karli

Sorry I emoted all over you as soon as you got back online. It was just so good to know you were there at the other end of an e-mail. Thanks a million for your lovely offer to chat on the phone, but I actually think I have myself sorted.

I've taken on board your comments re: the Peter-Patrick blow-up, and I'm prepared to admit that I may have (slightly) overreacted. I can see now that I didn't handle my disappointment very maturely, but I can't go back and change anything, so…

Whatever.

I'm over it, and I'm moving on. I'd like to think I've learned from the experience.

I've written to Patrick—not to apologise—I don't think that's called for—but to reopen communication. He's back on Magnetic Island and we are now exchanging polite and friendly (enough) e-mails. We're house-swappers again. Nothing more. Drama over.

I may yet take myself down to Cornwall. Yes, I know it could rub salt into my gradually healing wounds, but I really do want to see more of England before I have to leave, and time's running out.

Thanks for being the best friend a girl could ask for.

Love to you and to Jimbo
Molly

Dear Molly

Greetings from Bodo. I do hope you're well, and having as good a time as I've been having here in Norway. Actually, I've joined the crew of an Australian yacht and I'm about to leave port. We're heading for Madeira, and then across the Atlantic to Barbados, where this boat will be chartered for Caribbean cruises.

I'm planning to hitch a ride home on another boat, travelling through the Panama and across the Pacific. You wouldn't like to join me, would you? Think of all those gorgeous Pacific Islands we'd visit on the way home.

I'm sending my mobile phone number, just in case.

Miss you, Molly.

Brad xxx

Molly's Diary, June 12th

If I had any common sense I would probably jump at Brad's offer. What an adventure to sail a yacht home across the Pacific—and with such a nice guy for company.

Problem is (apart from the time it would take), I've lived on an island in the Pacific all my life, so that trip doesn't sound nearly as exotic and exciting to me as it would to a New South Wales sheep farmer. And while Brad's nice...he...well, there are times when nice isn't quite enough. And yet it should be, shouldn't it? Nice is safe. Nice doesn't break your heart.

I hope I'm not going to be one of those women who always falls for the wrong guys.

To: Patrick Knight <patrick.knight@mymail.com>
From: Molly Cooper <molly.cooper@flowermail.com>
Subject: It's a boy!

Dear Patrick

Rafael Felipe Azevedo was born last night at three minutes past midnight. This morning Cidalia insisted that I go with her to the hospital. (She's so proud. She wanted to show him off, and her daughter Julieta was very well and happy to receive visitors.)

I don't usually get too excited about babies—but, honestly, Patrick, have you ever seen a Brazilian baby? Truly, Rafael is so cute, with a cap of dark hair, the darkest, shiniest little black eyes, and the sturdiest, kicking limbs. He looks just like his father, and that's saying something. Now I know why Brazilian men have such a reputation for their good-looks.

By the way, I have made an executive decision and told Cidalia not to worry about cleaning your place this week. I can easily run around with a vacuum cleaner, and I'm sure you'll agree she deserves the time off.

Best wishes
Molly

To: Patrick Knight <patrick.knight@mymail.com>
From: Molly Cooper <molly.cooper@flowermail.com>

Subject: RE: It's a boy!

Dear Patrick

Cidalia has asked me to pass on her deepest thanks. She was absolutely thrilled with the beautiful flowers and the card you sent her. She said it's the first time a man has ever sent her flowers, and she was a little bit weepy. So thank you from me, too. It was very sweet of you, and I wish you could have seen the joy on her face.

Julieta, the proud new mother, is also thrilled with the baby boy gift hamper you sent. She can't believe you were so generous, and she asked me to thank you (although she will also write), and to tell you that she feels like a celebrity mum.

So you see, you're quite the man of the moment here, Patrick. I hope all's well with you, and that your new book idea is firing.

Best wishes

Molly

To: Patrick Knight: <patrick.knight@mymail.com>
From: Felicity Langley: <flissL@mymail.com>
Subject: Home again

Dear Patrick

How are you, darling? I hope you're enjoying the rest of your time on the island. It won't be all that long till you're back home again. The time seems to have gone very quickly, doesn't it?

As you can imagine, Jonathan and I had the most wonderful time in Italy, and we're now having fun planning to set up house. We've decided to sell both our old places and to start all over again with a home of our own. Honestly, we're having such a good time you'd think we were giddy young twenty-year-olds.

Speaking of houses, I called in at your place yesterday to see Molly, and I must say I was a little concerned. I thought she looked pale, and as if she'd lost weight. I don't suppose it's anything to worry about, just that her Australian tan has faded, and along with it some of her sparkle.

I'd assumed that you'd caught up with her while you were in London for the wedding, and I said something along those lines to Molly. Obviously I chose the wrong moment, or the wrong words. The poor girl had offered me a cup of tea, and she was reaching into a cupboard when I asked the question. Somehow I startled her, and she dropped two teacups and their saucers.

I know you won't be upset about the breakages. You tend to use coffee mugs anyhow. But poor Molly was very distressed. In a bid to calm her I suggested we forget tea and raid your drinks cabinet.

But, although Molly was almost her old self after a nice chat over a couple of gin and tonics, I noticed that she still avoided talking about you, Patrick. Apart from admitting that the two of you had met, she was strangely silent. If I didn't know you better I'd suggest that you might have blotted your copybook somehow.

As you know, I've been very impressed by the interesting young woman who's occupying your house. And I'm inordinately proud of you, darling, so I was hoping to hear positive comments about you from Molly.

Perhaps I'm being over-sensitive, but her reluctance to talk about you bothered me. I sensed unhappiness—which might have been caused by any number of things. I sincerely trust it's in no way connected to you.

Anyway, on a brighter note, Molly's planning a trip to Cornwall, which I think is a very good idea. Perhaps all she needs is to get out of London for a bit.

I look forward to hearing your news.

Love

Mother

To: Felicity Langley <flissL@mymail.com>
From: Patrick Knight: <patrick.knight@my-mail.com>
Subject: Re: Home again
Dear Mother
Thanks for your e-mail. It was good to hear from you, and to know that you and Jonathan are both so happy. I wish you luck with the buying and selling of your houses. Do keep me posted.

As for Molly…you're as astute as ever, and you're quite right. She's a wonderful woman, and unfortunately I did make a hash of meeting her.

I promise my intentions were honourable—dare I say chivalrous?—but I'm afraid my delivery backfired.

I'll spare you the details. Knowing your tender heart, you'll want to go round there and try to smooth things over, but I don't think that's wise.

I know you're concerned, but please don't worry. Molly and I are still in contact. We're not bitter enemies or anything like that.

Concentrate on Jonathan. At least you two have got it right.

Loads of love
Patrick

Private Writing Journal, June 15th

I can't bear to think that Molly's pale and losing weight because of me. Ever since my mother's e-mail I haven't been able to think of anything else. I need to make amends with Molly, but how?

I think a phone call's necessary. The worst she can do is hang up on me.

Molly's Diary, June 15th

Cornwall is so quaint!

I'm having two days away (midweek—can't afford to give up any more of my weekend shifts), and I can't believe how beautiful it is down here.

I mean, I've seen pictures of the English countryside before, so I don't suppose I should be surprised, but I thought there might just be the occasional little patch of quaintness. I've found old-world, picturesque charm everywhere.

I never imagined that so many cute and pretty little cottages actually existed. On the train journey down from London (leaving from Paddington), I saw whole villages of cottages—cottages with window boxes filled with flowers, or with roses climbing over the door, and cottages with proper, steep thatched

*roofs and little white-framed windows peep-
ing out like eyes from beneath a fringe of
thick hair.*

*I've seen the greenest of green, green fields,
divided by low drystone walls, and sheep that
are actually white—not dusty brown like ours
in Australia. And there are wildflowers blos-
soming everywhere—beside the roads, filling
little woodsy valleys, and poking out from
piles of rocks or from crannies in the walls.*

*I'm so glad I've come down to Cornwall,
even though I didn't come here in a British
racing-green sports car with a gorgeous man
at the wheel. The countryside is divine, and
I realise now that after the excitement and
busyness of London I've missed fresh air
and wide open spaces and the straightfor-
ward simplicity of the outdoors. Here there
are mountains in the distance, and moors,
and villages huddled on cliffs—and the sea!
Even palm trees.*

*Gosh, it almost made me homesick to smell
the briny, sharp scent of the sea and to see
the straggly fronds of palm trees.*

*I also got a bit weepy thinking about the
romantic weekend that never happened. As
a matter of fact I'm thinking about it far too
much as I nibble on a Cornish pasty while*

making my way up and down steep cobbled streets that cling to the edge of cliffs, or when I'm lying on the soft green grass of a cliff-top, looking down into the most astonishingly beautiful cove.

Yes, it's sad, but true—I'm wishing that Patrick was here beside me. Pathetic, isn't it? To be thinking so much about that wonderful weekend that I/we threw away?

I hope I don't sound as if I've changed my mind about Patrick. I haven't. I'm still super, super mad with him for pretending to be Peter. But in spite of all that I just know I would have loved our romantic weekend in Cornwall. It would have been something to remember for the rest of my life.

Even if I'm married at some time in the future, and have my own family, I'd still be able to look back on that memory of a happy, reckless, utterly romantic weekend in my youth.

Instead, I sit here on the bed in my B&B and look out through the window at a small sailing boat zipping briskly out across the bay, and I try so hard just to enjoy this moment—the beautiful view, the soft afternoon light, the scents of the sea, the familiar call of seagulls—but I feel dreadfully, horribly lonely.

I admit it. I'm deadbeat hopeless. Because now I'm actually imagining Patrick lying here on this bed beside me. I can see him...

He's lying on top of the white cotton bed-spread and his shirt is undone, revealing his gorgeous, broad, manly chest and his tight, flat abs. (These last details are not just fig-ments of my imagination. Thanks to Karli, who's seen him at the beach, I know they're true.) My wicked imagination adds a trail of dark hair disappearing beneath his jeans.

His dark brown eyes are watching me, and they're smoky and serious with desire. He reaches out and touches my arm, lightly, and I know exactly what's going to happen next. My skin flushes wherever he touches.

Then his fingertips touch my lips, and next minute I'm kissing his fingers, taking them into my mouth and grazing his nails with my teeth. I feel so turned on.

'Come here,' he whispers, and his voice is deep and husky and I'm wilting with longing.

I lean into him, and I smell him, and I can't hold back a soft, needy sigh. I'm so ready. I know we're about to make love. Beautiful, emotional, sensuous, love. Out-of-this world, amazing, mind-blowing love.

In the afternoon.

OK. OK. OK. OK. OK. OK.

Enough!

I can't believe I just wrote that fantasy into my diary. It proves I am now officially an idiot.

A certified idiot, filled with regrets. And anger.

Yes, I'm still red-hot angry. I'm mad with both Patrick and with myself. Why did he have to pretend to be someone he wasn't? And why did I have to overreact?

Why did we both have to throw everything away when it seemed pretty clear we had masses of potential for happiness?

Molly's Diary, June 17th

Oh, my God. Another disaster!

I am not exaggerating. This is The Very Worst Tragedy of My Entire Life!

I'm back in London and I'm curled in the foetal position in abject horror. The most terrible letter arrived in the mail while I was away. The postman must have slipped it through the front door slot on Saturday morning, and I found it lying on the mat in the

*hall—a letter addressed to me and forwarded
by Patrick from Australia.*

*At first I thought it was no big deal, but
now I've read the contents and I'm so sick.*

*Oh, help! I feel so stressed about this I
think I might actually throw up.*

ALC Assured Loans
Fieldstone House
George Street
Brisbane

Miss M.E. Cooper
32 Sapphire Bay Road
Magnetic Island
QLD 4819

Dear Miss Cooper

Following the purchase of the former
Northern Home and Building Co-operative
by our company, ALC Assured Loans, we are
now holders of the mortgage on a property at
32 Sapphire Bay Road, Magnetic Island—Lot
216, Parish of Cook—which is listed in your
name.

We regret to inform you that the loan repayments on this property are in arrears to
the sum of $5,450.69.

As holders of the mortgage, our company, ALC Assured Loans, has the right to foreclose on this loan and recover the outstanding amount of $46,300 in full.

To avoid this foreclosure you are required to make full payment of the arrears by June 10th.

J P Swan
Client services and recovery manager

Molly's Diary, June 17th

It's June seventeenth.

And they were demanding payment by June tenth!

Oh, help! I have no idea how this has happened, but the letter must have arrived on the island while Patrick was in England. When he got back he forwarded it to me, but it's taken another week to reach this address, and I've been in Cornwall.

I still can't believe it! I've always been so careful with my money, and paying off the mortgage has always been my top priority. I've already made one horrible trip to the bathroom, but I'm still sick with terror. That's why my handwriting is so shaky.

I don't understand this.

I can't cope with it. Pandanus Cottage isn't just my ticket to a secure future; I love that house. My grandparents bought it soon after they were married and it's the only home I've ever known. It may be humble, but it has million dollar views. I couldn't bear to lose it.

Accck! I've just checked my bank account on the internet and now I can see that the money for the repayments hasn't been taken out. No wonder I've been managing so well in London.

But how did this happen? I arranged the monthly transfers before I left Australia. What's gone wrong?

And why hasn't Patrick contacted me about this? I need to know what's happened. Has a debt collector landed on his doorstep? Has he been thrown out of my home? Oh, help, could anything worse happen during a house swap? I can't stand not knowing what's going on. I'm going to have to ring him.

It's two in the afternoon, so it's midnight in Queensland. I should probably wait till this evening to ring Patrick, but I think there's every danger that I will have perished from fright by then. And I can't ring the finance company. There won't be anyone in their of-

fices now. I have to ring Patrick. I hope he'll understand.

Oh, no. As soon as I went to the telephone I realised there were messages. From Patrick:

'Hi Molly. It's Patrick here. Could you ring me back when you get in?'

'Hi Molly. It's Patrick again. Obviously you're still not home. I'll try again later.'

I'm ashamed to admit that in spite of my overwhelming fear and terror I had the tiniest swoon when I heard Patrick's voice. He really does have the loveliest, most refined accent. And I know this sounds crazy, but just hearing his voice made me feel a little bit calmer.

And he was ringing from my home phone, so that's one good thing. At least when he left those messages yesterday he hadn't been kicked out.

CHAPTER ELEVEN

RING, ring...

Patrick fought to block out the telephone. It was dragging him from deep sleep and threatening his blissful dream.

He was in Cornwall with Molly, and there was no way he wanted to wake up.

Molly was standing at the edge of a cliff, drawing in deep breaths of sea air. Her hair was wind-blown and wonderfully tangled, and she was wearing a dark green skirt that hugged her neat hips, and a white blouse with long sleeves made from something soft, with ruffles at her throat and her wrists. A pirate's shirt.

The wind pressed the soft fabric against her body, outlining the slimness of her waist and the sweet, tempting roundness of her breasts.

She turned to him and smiled. Her cheeks were pink from the sea air and her eyes sparkled with warmth, like sudden sunshine. Her arms opened to him and he hurried forward, his heart light and floating with the most amazing happiness.

Ring, ring...

No, please no. Not now. Molly was almost in his arms.

Ring, ring.

The phone nagged at Patrick, but he refused to move. Hadn't he read somewhere that dreams vanished when you moved? Besides, who would call at this time of night?

The answer came in a flash.

Molly. She would be calling from London, worried about her house.

He sat up, heart racing, and snatched up the phone from the bedside table. 'Hello?'

'Patrick? It's Molly.'

'Hi. How are you?'

'I'm very relieved to hear your voice, actually.'

He smiled in the darkness, pleased she could say that in spite of everything that had gone wrong between them.

She said, 'I assume you can't have been kicked out of the cottage if you're answering this phone?'

'Of course I'm still here.'

'I was worried because of the letter you forwarded. Did you know it was from the loan company who hold my mortgage?'

'Yes. But don't worry, Molly.'

'I can't help worrying. Have they contacted you at all?'

'They sent someone round here yesterday. He tried to serve foreclosure papers.'

'Oh, God.' Her voice trembled with terror. 'So they really are going to take my house away from me?'

'No, they aren't. They can't. They haven't a chance. Don't panic. I've sorted it out.' Patrick spoke soothingly, anxious to allay her fears. He knew how much she loved this house, and after the major emotional problems he'd created for her he hated that this had happened as well.

Under any other circumstances he might have seized this chance to apologise for the hash he'd made of things in London, but her fears for her home were more important.

'Patrick, what do you mean you've sorted it out? How could you?'

'Very easily. I'm a banker, remember?'

'Well, yes, that's true. But how did you manage it?'

'As I said, the loan company sent someone round. An islander called Ross Fink. Apparently he knows you?'

'Oh, yes. Everyone knows everyone on the island. Ross delivers parcels from the ferry. Gosh, he's such a sweet guy. I had no idea he was a debt collector.'

'Actually he was worried, because he knew you were away. So I sat him down, and got his end of the story, and then I asked him to wait while I rang the loan company in Brisbane to get to the bottom of the problem.'

'Gosh, Patrick. That's—that's wonderful.'

'It's no big deal. It's the kind of thing I do all the time.' Just the same, he couldn't help being warmed by the awe and respect in Molly's voice. 'They put me through to Jason Swan, the recovery manager, and I told him I was acting on your behalf. I explained my background in banking, and that I know how the system works, and I urged him not to proceed.'

'Really?' She sounded astonished, as if he'd accomplished a miracle.

'I told him he'd find himself in a legal mess that would cost him more than it's worth. Then I explained that you were overseas, and there'd been delays with forwarding the mail. I assured him that if he gave me his firm's account details the money would be transferred immediately.'

'Immediately?' There was an audible gasp on the other end of the line. 'But—but I couldn't pay. I've been in Cornwall.'

'It's OK, Molly. As I said, it's all settled.'

'You don't mean you've paid my debt?'

'It was a simple matter.' Patrick tried to make light

of it. He knew how fiercely independent Molly was, and he didn't want this to become a big issue.

'It's—it's very kind of you, Patrick. Amazing. Thank you so much. But it's hardly a simple matter. I owed over five thousand dollars.' Molly had sounded stunned, but now she sounded worried again. 'I'll pay you back straight away. If you tell me where you'd like the money deposited—'

'Don't worry about that now. The problem's over. We can sort out the details later.'

'How much later? I hate being in debt.'

Patrick suppressed a sigh. 'That's very commendable, Molly, but you should hang onto your money for the rest of your time in England. You never know when you might need it, and you only have a couple of weeks left to enjoy the sights. You should splash out and make sure you see all the things you really want to see.'

She tried several more times to protest, but he held her at bay. He even tried to make a joke of it. 'I don't mind having a short-term investment in a lovely place like Pandanus Cottage.'

'The thing is,' she said eventually, 'I don't understand how this happened. I set up an automatic transfer. The money should have been going through.'

Patrick assured her that this kind of hiccup wasn't unusual. Human error or computer glitches could cause unexpected problems. A form had been misplaced. Someone had left a digit off an account number.

'The ALC company's dodgy, though,' he said. 'They were far too quick to jump on you to foreclose. They didn't give you nearly enough warning.'

'I continued using my gran's mortgage company,' Molly said. 'But it looks as if they've been taken over by this new crowd.'

He suggested she should use a reputable bank, and she promised to look into it just as soon as she got home.

She thanked him. Effusively. And he realised with a thud of alarm that their conversation might end at any moment.

He was grappling to think of a suitable question when Molly asked, 'How's your book progressing?'

Surprised, Patrick answered honestly. 'Really well. I'm writing twelve, fourteen, sometimes seventeen hours a day.'

'Wow. You're really burning the midnight oil.'

Patrick grinned ruefully. 'I guess I'm crazy to be working so hard when I'm on holiday on this beautiful island, but I want to have a rough draft finished before I leave.'

'Well, good for you.' Her voice was warm and genuine. Almost the old Molly. 'So what's the new story about now that you've dropped Beth Harper and the MI5?'

'You'll never believe this.'

'Why? You're not writing a novel about two people who swap houses, are you?'

'No, no—nothing like that. It's perfectly safe non-fiction. A step-by-step guide for Generation Y on how to manage their finances.'

'Oh, dear.'

Patrick's mind whirred as he searched for a fresh conversation topic. The last thing he wanted was to waste precious time talking about himself.

'How was your trip to Cornwall?' he asked quickly, but as soon as the question was out he was drenched with ridiculous memories of his dream. Of Molly's bright smile and her open arms, the deep ruffles on her white blouse, the soft fabric clinging to her perfect shape.

To make matters worse, his question was met by silence.

'Molly?' He wondered if he'd been so distracted by his fantasy that he'd missed her reply. 'Are you still there?'

'Yes.' Her answer was scarcely more than a tiny bleat.

'Did you like Cornwall?'

'Y-yes. It—it was l-lovely.'

Hell. He'd upset her. He'd raised a touchy subject and no doubt made her angry again.

Idiot, idiot, idiot.

'Um—while we're on the phone,' she said quickly,

as if she couldn't wait to change the subject, 'I suppose we should talk about our return dates. Are your plans still firm? Will you be leaving Australia on the thirtieth?'

'Oh.' He struggled to drag his mind away from totally inappropriate images of himself and Molly in a cosy B&B in Cornwall. 'I—I haven't checked with the airlines, but I don't imagine anything's changed.'

'Good. I don't plan to make any changes either. So I guess we'll pass each other somewhere over the Indian Ocean?'

He felt a sinking feeling of cold despair. 'I dare say we shall.'

'But right now I'm keeping you up in the middle of the night,' she said matter-of-factly, 'so I'd better let you get back to bed.'

'Well, OK,' Patrick agreed, reluctantly accepting that Molly was anxious to get off the line. 'It's been great to talk to you, Molly.' He added this with heartfelt sincerity.

The phone call ended and Patrick sat in the dark, on the edge of Molly's bed, wide awake, listening to the silence of the house and the distant soft slap of waves on the beach.

Once again Molly was giving out loud and clear signals. She wasn't giving him *any* chance to resume or restore their relationship.

For the first time since he'd arrived on the island he felt desperately lonely.

Molly's Diary, June 17th

I'm feeling quite a bit calmer now. I've spoken to Patrick in person, and I'm still shaken and stirred, but definitely calmer.

I must say that I couldn't have chosen a better person to swap houses with than a banking expert and financial diplomat.

My phone call woke him up, of course, and he sounded understandably sleepy. I think he was yawning when he picked up the phone, but as soon as he realised I was the caller he woke up properly. And then I couldn't believe how kind and calm and take-charge he was.

He spoke with such quiet authority I began to breathe more easily straight away, and I felt safer. In truth I was awestruck by this very in-control banker side of Patrick.

Perhaps it's just as well he's in Australia, because if he'd been within arm's length of me I would have hugged him and kissed him—which is hardly wise after the way we parted.

The one bad thing was the way he wouldn't let me clear my debt immediately. He kept insisting there was no hurry. But I owe him five thousand, four hundred and fifty dollars and sixty-nine cents!

Perhaps he wasn't keen to give his banking details over the phone. In the end I gave up. For now. It was either that or have another argument with him, and I didn't want to fight when he'd been so kind and helpful.

But then he asked me about Cornwall, and I couldn't believe how stupidly tongue-tied I suddenly became. It should have been so easy to talk about two days in southwest England—like reciting a travelogue—but I was swamped with all kinds of emotions.

I couldn't help thinking about what might have been.

And, heaven help me, I started blushing, as if Patrick could read my mind and knew I'd been thinking about the silly fantasy I recorded in my diary—of him stretched out on the white bed in the Cornish B&B.

What would he have thought if he'd known that I was picturing his shirt falling temptingly open to reveal the dark breadth of his chest? Or that I was feeling his hand touching me, his fingers tracing the shape of my lips? And more.

Thank heavens fantasies are private affairs.

We got over that awkward moment, and I thanked him again profusely. But, honestly, I must be a terrible ingrate.

There I was, incredibly indebted to Patrick—he'd saved my home and lifted an enormous worry from my shoulders—and yet I still felt unsettled and vaguely unhappy as I hung up the phone.

Molly's Diary, June 18th

Today I've stopped angsting about the money I owe Patrick, because I'm beginning to see that he might be right. It's certainly nice to have plenty of funds for my last week and a bit in London. I've made a list of all the things I'd like to do before I go home, and unfortunately many of them involve spending money.

Things to do before I leave London:

1. Buy two replacement fine bone china tea-cups and matching saucers (NB not flowery ones).
2. Buy souvenir gifts for my friends on the island—especially for Karli and Jimbo. And for Jill, who's been filling in for me at the

Sapphire Bay resort. OK, something small for Jodie G and her progeny.

3. Buy a thank-you/house-warming present for Patrick's mother, who's been so very kind.

4. Buy a round or two of farewell drinks for my workmates at the Empty Bottle.

5. Visit the National Portrait Gallery one more time. I've already been there twice, but I need another chance to take in the faces of all those famous people—everyone from Richard III to the Beatles.

6. Splash out on a haircut and styling at a really good London salon. After living in trendy London for so long, I want to go home looking fabulous!

I think that's all. Thing is, I'm out and about so much now, using every moment of my spare time, that I hardly have a moment to write in my diary. Which is a very good thing, of course. If I stop to think too much my thoughts head down a dead-end street straight towards a certain Englishman...

I remember how close he is to my ideal Englishman...and how hard it is to accept that the only way I've ever known the real Patrick is through e-mails. The man I met

*was acting a part, but he knew me so well
through my e-mails that he knew what but-
tons to press.*

*Put on a suit, play the gentleman, take her
to Covent Garden.*

*I think about the fun we might have had if
Patrick had been up-front and open—the fun
we never could have now.*

*But here's the thing that's been worrying
me most…keeping me awake at night and
stealing my appetite. Now that Patrick's
saved my house, I can't help seeing it as one
deliberately kind act in a series of acts of
deliberate kindness.*

*Right from the very start Patrick Knight
has been kind and thoughtful. He sent me
the book about London's secrets. He sent his
mother round to help me get over my fear
of the Underground. He sent lovely gifts to
Cidalia and Julieta. And—most importantly,
perhaps—he effectively rescued my cottage.*

*It seems that whenever I've needed some-
thing Patrick's been there for me. And when
I think about that I can't help seeing that the
whole Peter debacle was almost certainly
Patrick again, trying to be kind.*

*Now that I have a little distance and per-
spective, and when I consider all the other*

*ways he's helped me, I can see that it makes
perfect sense that he would try to help me
with the one thing I claimed to want more
than anything else—my dream date with an
English gentleman.*

*If that's true, the angry way I behaved must
have come across as terribly rude and un-
grateful to Patrick.*

*Then I remember his kiss, which could
not by any stretch of the imagination be described as an act of kindness. That kiss was
all about hot-blooded lust. No doubt about
it. I was introduced to Patrick's inner cave
man—and it was incredibly exciting, thrilling, intoxicating...*

*Until he remembered he was playing the
role of a gentleman. And he retreated. Only
to ring the next morning with the Cornwall
plan.*

*Thinking about all of this, I'm overcome
with shame for my rash and angry response.
I'm drowning in if-onlys...*

*Not just if only we'd gone to Cornwall. But
if only I'd been just a little more sympathetic
when Patrick was offering his explanation....
If only I hadn't jumped in with guns blaz-
ing, slamming the door and sending back his
flowers and refusing to phone him.*

All that time I was smugly thinking I was in the right.

If only I could tell him I've shifted in my thinking and I'd like to apologise.

If only I could see him one more time.

But it's not going to happen, and I can't live my life weighed down by if-onlys and what-ifs.

To: Molly Cooper <molly.cooper@flowermail. com>
From: Karli Henderson <hendo86@flower-mail.com>
Subject: Your Patrick!

Hi Molly

I hope you're making the most of your final days in London. Hasn't the time flown? I wish I was going to be on the island to welcome you home.

I hear that the islanders are planning a huge farewell party for your house swapper, so it seems that for a quiet man Patrick's become a big hit.

I understand Jodie G is going to make the most of this party, and will have one last stab at trying to win Patrick's attention/heart/body. (Take your pick. She's not fussy.) You have to hand it to that girl—she never gives up. I don't suppose you'll mind what happens between them now, so that's one good thing.

I wonder if you've developed a taste for travel? Maybe you'll decide to keep house swapping. I can see you in Tuscany, or on a Greek Island. Let me know if you decide to swap with someone from Las Vegas.

Seriously, Mozza, have a safe journey home. I'll try to get back to the island as soon as I can—or you're very welcome to visit us here, if you don't mind sleeping on the sofa. You must know I'm dying to see you.

Love you heaps

Karli

Molly's Diary, June 24th

OK, I've made a decision. A very big decision. Huge.

It all came from thinking constantly about my unfinished business with Patrick. Not just my financial debt, which is bad enough, but my feeling of being out on an emotional limb with no safe place to settle.

The last time I saw Patrick I was confused and disappointed, and I never gave him a chance to explain his behaviour. We didn't talk, which is crazy, because I love to talk.

Now, if I want to make amends, I think it's up to me.

My plan, therefore, (quite brilliant, actually) will allow me to kill two birds with one stone.

Instead of going back to Australia without seeing Patrick again I'm going to change my flight, delaying it by four hours, so I'll still be here in London when he arrives. Then I propose to talk to him about everything, and make peace with him, and hand over a cheque for the money I owe him. Thus all debts and issues will be settled.

NB This has nothing to do with Karli's suggestion that Jodie Grimshaw might win Patrick's attention at the farewell party on the island. If he was going to fall for Jodie it would have happened ages ago.

I'll meet Patrick at Heathrow, and I'll be calm and polite and ladylike and mature (and hopefully I'll also look ravishing, with my new hairstyle from Edgar's in Soho), and Patrick and I will be able to have the conversation we should have had weeks ago.

I know it's too late to change the past, or to try to revisit it. We won't take off for Cornwall or anything wonderfully crazy like that. But at least my conscience will be clear and...

I don't know...

I guess I'll be able to get on with the rest of my life.

Now the decision is made I feel so much better.

Private Writing Journal, June 29th

I can't believe my time here is over.

There are so many, many things about this island that I'm going to miss—the views through the trees to the bright sparkling blue sea, the towering, scrub-covered mountains and the rocky bays, the palm trees and the sandy beaches, so white and gold. I'll miss the little rock wallabies scampering about, even in the backyards and public places, and the bright, squabbling parrots that come to my balcony to be fed.

I've also grown so used to the silence here that I'm sure I'm going to miss it. I've become accustomed to the occasional sounds of nature—the bird-calls at sunrise and the buzzing of cicadas in the gum trees at sunset, the chattering of fruit bats in the mango tree... There are almost no man-made sounds.

Now, too late, I wish I'd explored more, taken more photographs, learned more about the trees, the plants and the original inhabitants...

I know I'll miss the friendly locals, with their laconic good humour and their laidback manner and their smiling, shoulder-shrugging reaction to everything.

When I get back to work at the bank (shudder) and old George Sims throws the first of his fits, I plan to simply turn to him with a slow grin and tell him, 'No worries, mate.'

The thing is, this is the worst time to leave a tropical island—in the middle of the glorious winter days. Molly was so right— this time of year is magical. Out of this world. The air is as clear and crisp as champagne, and although the temperature is cooler it's so sunny I long to abandon my desk and go for long walks, or to swim from one end of the bay to the other.

Each evening at dusk the sky and the sea and the tops of the hills are tinged with a magenta blush.

It's another world.

If Molly was here with me...

It would be Paradise.

Molly's Diary, June 30th

I've been through such a seesaw of emotions

during this past week. I'm so sad about leaving London and leaving the friends that I've made here—all the people at work, as well as Cidalia and her lovely family, and Patrick's wonderful mum.

But now my suitcases are packed and groaning once again, and I've said my goodbyes to my favourite London people and to my favourite London places. I've given and received gifts. I've eaten farewell dinners and downed farewell drinks. I've returned Patrick's key to the safety deposit box at the bank around the corner on the King's Road. And I've wept.

OK, I'm not going to write about how often I've wept, because I might come across as a complete watering pot, or I might get teary again, and I need to be dry-eyed and smiling today. I'm already at Heathrow, you see.

This evening I travelled to the airport in a square black London taxi through the rain. The roads were shiny and wet, reflecting all the streetlights and the neon signs. It was quite magical, really, to see all that shiny black bitumen streaked with shimmering splashes of yellow, red, green and blue. I think there's something extraordinarily beautiful but sad about a city on a rainy night—especially when you're dry in the back of a comfortable taxi cab and you're leaving, and you know you will almost certainly never be coming back.

In a few hours' time I'll be flying home.

But right now I don't want to think about that. I'm in the Arrivals lounge, and I can see on the huge screen above the doorway that Patrick's plane has just—at this very moment—landed.

Squee! Just writing that he's here makes my heart leap like a nervous kitten. His plane is somewhere out there on the Heathrow tarmac, taxiing into its gate, and I'm practically exploding with excitement.

I know I'm taking a big risk by surprising him like this, but I've practised what I have to say a thousand times and I really feel it needs to be said. Face to face.

Oh, help. Now I just have to get it right.

Of course it's going to be ages yet before I see Patrick. First he has to get through Customs and Immigration, and then he has to collect his baggage, and he's going to be tired and jet-lagged, and he won't be expecting me, so the whole situation is fraught. I'm trying to stay calm, but it's very hard.

I thought writing in my diary might help.

It's not helping.

I've been to the Ladies' twice already to check my clothes and to touch-up my make-up, and—yes, I should be honest—to admire my new hairstyle. Edgar's in Soho has given me an amazing new look. Now, instead of tight brown corkscrews, I have soft, silky curls that bounce.

'It's all about using the right products,' Edgar explained.

So I'm going home to Australia armed with vitamin-enriched lotions, deep conditioners and a daily spritz. Although once I'm back on Magnetic Island the tropical humidity will have its wicked way, and before long I'll probably give up trying to look glamorous....

OK, it's now half an hour since Patrick's plane landed, so he should be moving through the tedious lines of travellers, gradually making his way towards this lounge. The place is teeming with people of every race and every age and in every kind of dress. There are people in Middle Eastern robes and Indian saris, and in pinstriped business suits and ripped jeans and T-shirts.

I have no idea what Patrick will be wearing. I'm suddenly terrified I might miss him. I didn't think it would be possible to miss seeing Patrick. Apart from the fact that he's so tall and dark and stand-out handsome, I was sure I'd have some kind of inbuilt sensor that would zero in on him and pick him out of millions. But now that I'm here in this vast sea of humanity I'm having doubts. I'm thinking that I should have warned him and arranged a proper meeting.

I have no choice but to stand as close as possible to the door that he has to come through. Surely I can't miss him there.

Still at Heathrow...

Another hour has passed and there's still no sign of Patrick. I know he hasn't walked through this door, and I think it's the only way he could have entered. I heard Aussie accents some time back, and so I asked a man what flight he was on and it was Patrick's flight. I did my best to remain calm after that. I stood by the door in eager anticipation, but Patrick hasn't appeared.

I can't have missed him. Not when I'm standing here, more or less on guard by the door. Unless there are other doors.

Oh, God, I have no idea where he is, and very soon I have to leave or I'll miss my plane. I've already paid an extra fee because

I've changed my flight once. I can't afford to change it again.

I'm worried. What can have happened? I refuse to consider the possibility that Jodie Grimshaw got her claws into Patrick at the farewell party and convinced him to stay with her and her hyperactive child. I can rise above such thoughts. I can. I can.

Just the same, I've forgotten every word of my rehearsed speech. I'm so sick with nerves that if I saw Patrick now I'd be a stammering mess. But I guess it doesn't really matter because I have to go.

My plan has failed. I have to pack up this diary and trudge over to Departures. I'm fighting tears.

My heart is a stone in my chest.

I know it's silly, but I can't help thinking about that scene in A Westminster Affair, *when Vanessa was riding off on a red double-decker bus, about to zoom out of Christian's life, but then she realised she was making a terrible mistake and that she would never see him again if she didn't act immediately.*

That's how I feel. I can't get on that plane until I've seen Patrick. But—

Where is he?

CHAPTER TWELVE

THE ferry bumped against the wharf at Nelly Bay, and the movement woke Molly.

Disorientated, she sat up, and when she peered through the window of the lower deck she saw barnacle-encrusted pylons and aqua-green water. Her nose wrinkled as she smelled the sharp salt of the sea mingled with the dank mustiness of seasoned timbers.

Lifting her gaze, she saw the familiar glass-fronted ferry terminal and a row of palm trees in giant pots. Beyond the terminal hills towered, studded with gumtrees and huge, smooth boulders, and arching above everything the bright blue sky was turning soft mauve as the afternoon slipped towards dusk.

She was home.

Safe on the island—*her* island.

She knew she should be happy, but this was the first time she'd come home to the island when neither her gran nor Karli was there to welcome her. And this homecoming was so much worse, because she'd left England without sighting Patrick. Her worry over where he might be had eaten at her like a nasty disease throughout the long flight back.

She still had no idea. At Brisbane airport she'd rung his home in Chelsea, but she'd only heard his answering machine, so she still didn't know if he'd missed his plane, if he'd been detained in transit, or if he was ill.

On top of those concerns her head ached and her neck had developed a crick from sleeping sitting up. Her limbs were leaden as she tried to stand.

After twenty-four hours of travelling, all she wanted was to crawl into bed and sleep for a week. No, a month.

She disembarked via a ramp which was steeper than usual because it was very low tide. Phil, one the ferry's attendants, had dumped her luggage on the wharf.

'How was London?' he asked.

'Fabulous.' She managed a weak smile, then wheeled her suitcases to the car park, where her old rust-bucket was waiting in the sun like a faithful puppy—exactly where Patrick had said he would leave it, with its key tucked inside the exhaust pipe.

Molly hefted her luggage into the boot and slammed the lid. Yawning deeply, she sagged behind the steering wheel and turned on the ignition, surprised that the motor didn't cough or splutter.

Winding down the window, she steered the car gently forward. The sea breeze played havoc with her hair as the ancient rattletrap chugged over the hill to Geoffrey Bay, then on through Arcadia and over the next hill to the bay after that.

From the crests of the hills Molly saw the tropical sea stretching out to the curving horizon. As always, the water at this time of day was silvergrey and tinged with lavender and pink—serene and cool and endless.

Looking at it, Molly felt her spirits lift. Momentarily. They quickly drooped again.

Perhaps in time…in a very long time…she would begin to feel like her old self. Or perhaps not.

Right now she was too tired and too emotionally flattened to feel anything close to happiness. She felt as limp as a balloon, forgotten in a corner after everyone had left the party.

At last she saw her little white cottage through the trees. She turned down the short dirt track that wound through the scrub and pulled into her carport. Then she struggled with her luggage, dragging it to the front door.

The key was under the flower pot, and as she retrieved it she couldn't help thinking that not so long ago Patrick's hand had placed it there.

Fool. I've got to stop thinking about him.

The front door opened on unexpectedly silent

hinges. Molly stepped inside, drew a deep breath, and looked about her. Her house was tidy, and it smelled clean. For a moment she fancied she could almost catch of whiff of Patrick's special scent.

How silly.

She drank in details. Amazingly, Patrick had put everything back in its right place, so that her house was exactly as she'd left it three months ago. He'd even left little handwritten notes dotted about the furniture.

Abandoning her bags on the doorstep, she hurried forward, eager to snatch up the nearest note propped against a pot plant in the middle of the dining table. She stared at Patrick's distinctive, spiky handwriting.

I've watered this plant and it's still alive. Note new growth—three new leaves and a bud. No water in saucer and no mossies.

Molly's mouth curved into a smile. She couldn't help it. She clutched the note against her suddenly thumping heart.

She turned to another note, stuck on the wall near the light switch.

Gecko lizard has had babies and they live behind the painting on this wall. Their names are Leonard, Zac and Elizabeth.

Molly's smile broadened, then wobbled as she felt a painful lump filling her throat. She went on to the next note in the kitchen.

This tap no longer leaks.

'Amazing,' she announced to the empty room. 'Patrick not only takes care of pot plants and geckos, he's also a plumber. The man's a legend.'

She was trying to sound sarcastic, to prove she wasn't moved, but she found herself stifling a sob. Dismayed, she whirled around, only to find yet another note stuck on the fridge.

Champagne and chocolates in here.

'Oh, Patrick, no.'

He was being kind. Again. Still. And she wasn't sure she could bear it. Not when she hadn't been able to see him, or speak to him, or say any of the things she'd wanted to tell him.

She opened the fridge and saw proper French Champagne and Belgian chocolate truffles. How on earth had Patrick found such exotic luxuries on this island? Molly's emotions threatened to overwhelm her.

It's just jet-lag, she decided as her mouth pulled out of shape. She pressed a fist against her lips. *I mustn't cry. Not tonight.*

If she started she might never stop.

Blinking hard, she retrieved her luggage from the doorstep and carried it purposefully through to her bedroom. Golden sunlight slanted into the darkened room through the bamboo blinds, tiger-striping the straw matting and her neatly made double bed—the bed Patrick had slept in until very recently.

There were two small squares of paper—two more notes—one on each pillow.

The first note said: *We need to talk, Molly.*

The other: *I have so much to tell you.*

Her heart leapt, beating hard and fast, like wings trying to hold her up in the air, but her knees were distinctly wobbly and she sank helplessly onto the edge of the bed.

What did the notes mean? Where could they talk? When? How?

Where *was* Patrick?

Her weariness had vanished, washed away by shock and by wonder and by the teensiest flicker of hope.

She couldn't help wondering if Patrick was as keen as she was to set things straight between them.

But that didn't mean…

That he…

Felt…

Oh, help. Molly's heart thrashed as she scanned the room, searching for more notes…

There was nothing that looked out of place, but the light was dim. Jumping to her feet she flicked the light switch.

No more messages.

Perhaps he'll send an e-mail, she thought. I mustn't get too worked up about a few Post-it notes. I should unpack. Be sensible. Make a cup of tea.

Instead she went to the white louvred French doors that led to the bathroom and pushed them open.

There was a note stuck on the mirror. It was longer than the others. In fact it looked like a list.

Almost afraid to read it, Molly stepped closer and her eyes flew down the page.

10 REASONS WHY I MUST SEE MOLLY AGAIN
  1. To tell her how sorry I am for stuffing things up in London.
  2. To try to explain that I would *never* willingly hurt her.
  3. To tell her that her e-mails have brightened my days.
  4. And my nights.
  5. To tell her that meeting her in person has changed me.
  6. That she's changed my life in vitally important ways.
  7. To tell her I need to kiss her again.

8. And again.
9. And again.
10. And again.

Now Molly was smiling and weeping at the same time.

The phone beside the bed began to ring, and she spun round, a hand pressed against the leaping pulse at her throat.

If the caller was one of the islanders she didn't think she could talk. She couldn't drum up cheery chatter about her holiday. Not tonight.

But if it was Patrick…

Could it be Patrick?

She picked up the phone carefully, as if it were a bomb about to explode. As she held it to her ear her insides danced as if she'd swallowed fireflies. 'Hello?'

'Oh, you're home at last.' His voice was deep and beautifully English. 'Welcome back.'

'Patrick?'

'How are you, Molly?'

He sounded as if he was smiling, and it was ridiculous but Molly felt instantly happy. Just hearing his lovely voice soothed her and excited her.

'I'm fine, thanks.' She was grinning from ear to ear.

'I thought you'd be home earlier.'

'I changed to a later flight.'

'Oh, I see. Have you settled in?'

'Not yet. I've only just arrived.' Feeling suddenly emboldened, she said, 'I've been busy tidying up all the mess here.'

'Mess?'

'Yes. Someone was staying here, you see, and he's left bits of paper all over the house.'

'Oh. How thoughtless… Some chaps are dashed untidy.'

'Aren't they just?'

An awkward silence fell, and Molly wondered if her little attempt at humour had fallen flat. Her confidence faltered.

'Patrick?'

'Yes?'

'I—I've seen the bathroom.'

'Oh, right,' he replied cautiously. 'Was it tidy?'

'It was particularly *un*tidy.'

After a beat, he said, 'Sounds like the fellow who's been staying at your place might need to apologise.'

'No apology necessary.' Molly swallowed. 'I—I loved the note.'

There was a shaky laugh and a huff of relief.

Molly's curiosity got the better of her. 'Where are you? I waited for you at Heathrow and you weren't on your flight.'

'You waited?'

'Yes, I wanted to talk to you. There was so much I wanted to tell you.'

'Oh, Molly.'

'What happened, Patrick? I couldn't find you.'

'I didn't catch the plane.'

'Really?' Shock riffled through her like a lightning strike. 'Why not?'

'I wanted to be here when you got back.'

'Here?'

'On the island. I'm on the beach right now, and I'm looking up through the trees to your house. I can see the light in your bedroom window.'

It was almost dusk, and the light was fading fast, but Molly fairly flew down the track to the beach. The path was steep, and at times rocky, and twice she almost tripped over tangled tree roots.

She reached the lower section quite quickly, and could see the smooth white sand ahead. And the darkening sea. And the tall, shadowy outline of a man.

Patrick.

He was coming across the sand towards her.

She began to run.

Now they were both running. Running towards each other. Arms outstretched.

And at last—

At last Patrick swept her into his arms. He was looking earnest and worried and yet extraordinarily relieved. She wanted to tell him all the things she had planned to say, but before she could speak he kissed her.

And so she kissed him back.

And it took a very long time.

They sat on the warm sand, watching the full moon rise out of the sea, a great golden disc of molten brilliance. Molly's head rested on Patrick's shoulder, and he knew his heart had never been fuller.

'I've made so many mistakes,' he said. 'But I think now that they were all preparation for this.' He brushed a corner of her brow with his lips. 'Have you any idea how long I've been in love with you?'

She appeared to give the question serious thought. 'Could it have started when you saw me in my black dress at Covent Garden?'

Patrick laughed.

'What's so funny? That's as glamorous as I get.'

'You looked beautiful that night, but I'd fallen long before then.'

'Tell me about it,' she said with an unabashed smile. 'I'm all ears.'

'Let me see...' Reaching an arm around her

shoulders, he hugged her. 'I think it more or less dawned on me when I was so ridiculously excited about going back to London for my mother's wedding. I mean, I was thrilled and happy for her and Jonathan, but I think I knew that a lot of my excitement was about wanting to meet you. Your e-mails were so open and honest. I loved your zest for life and your thirst for adventure and I wanted to share it.'

'So it had nothing to do with the way I looked?'

'Are you joking, Molly?'

'Tell me. A girl likes to hear these things.'

Patrick was aware that he'd never been very forthcoming with compliments, but with Molly it was incredibly easy. 'Actually, I was in lust with the photo you left on your fridge,' he confessed. 'I spent hours and hours, when I was supposed to be writing, staring at your legs, or trying to work out the colour of your eyes. And then I met the real thing and I was a lost man.'

Molly grinned, and her blue eyes sparkled, and she leaned in and rewarded him with another lovely kiss. 'So I'm to blame for ruining your novel?'

'Not really. That fault was all mine. I'm not very good at fiction.' Patrick frowned, aware that he needed to broach a very important subject. 'Molly, can you forgive me for pulling the Peter Kingston stunt?'

'Of course,' she said, surprisingly calm. 'I'm sorry I made such a stink. That's the big thing I waited at Heathrow to tell you. I realised you were just being kind.' She turned to look at him with a direct and clear gaze. 'That's right, isn't it?'

'It was partly that—about trying to give you your fantasy.' Patrick looked at the rising moon, which had cast a silver path across the sea almost to their feet. 'But you had such high expectations, and I wasn't sure I'd measure up on my own. It seemed safer, somehow, to hide behind a mask. I foolishly assumed that you'd understand.'

'I understand now.' She laid a gentle hand on his arm. 'But you shouldn't have worried. Patrick Knight has so much more going for him than Peter Kingston.'

'Tell me why,' he said, smiling with relief. 'I'm all ears.'

'Well, to start with, Patrick Knight lives in my favourite city in the whole world.'

'There's that, I guess.'

'And he has a wonderful mother—someone I already look on as a friend.'

'She adores you.'

'And he likes my island.'

'He does. He loves it.'

'I should possibly also mention the fireworks in my veins every time I look at him.'

'Molly…'

'And the fact that he's so sweet.'

'Sweet?'

Molly smiled. 'Don't look so surprised. Patrick Knight is very kind and thoughtful. He sent me a book about London, and ever since he's gone out of his way to make me happy. I've learned so much from him about the world beyond this little island, about my father, about myself.' She pressed her nose against his neck. 'And then there's the way he smells. It drives me wild.' Her lips grazed his jaw seductively. 'Would you like to know the best thing?'

He gave a choked little laugh. 'Sure.'

'Patrick's not always a perfect English gentleman. I have the distinct impression that I'm going to love his inner cave man.'

With a cry somewhere between laughter and longing, Patrick jumped to his feet, reached down and scooped Molly into his arms.

'You can't carry me,' she gasped. 'Not all the way to the cottage.'

'I can try.'

'No need. Put me down and let's run.'

EPILOGUE

To: Patrick Knight <patrick.knight@mymail.com>
From: Molly Cooper <molly.cooper@flower-mail.com>
Subject: My first love letter

Dearest Patrick

By now you will be safely home in Chelsea. I hope you had a comfortable journey and that everything was just as it should be at 34 Alice Grove.

I'm sure you can guess that I'm missing you already, but I'm determined not to moan. How can I complain when I've had you all to myself for two whole, perfectly blissful weeks?

I'm thrilled that you broke your lifelong habit of hard work so you could devote all that time just to me. It was two weeks of heaven, and I'm honoured to know that this was one of the vitally important changes you wanted to make in your life—taking time out, not working, not writing a book. Just being.

With me.

I must admit that when you handed me your journal with that cute, shy smile of yours and said you'd like me to read it, I was a bit stunned. That's a pretty big step for a guy, and I was very nervous about letting you read everything I'd written in my diary (especially about my trip to Cornwall).

But it was actually very liberating to share such complete and intimate honesty, wasn't it? No wonder we felt so wonderfully close by the end of our two weeks—as if we'd known each other all our lives.

Now that you're home again, Patrick, it's time for me to get busy with planning for September. It was so sweet of you to insist on having our wedding here on the island.

I couldn't think of anything more perfect than to be married to you on the beach at sunset. But to be honest, my darling, I would have married you anywhere—even in a Tube station. As for our honeymoon in Cornwall—you know how over the moon I am about that.

Next week I'm heading up to Cairns, to spend a few days with Karli and Jimbo. Of course I want to show off my gorgeous engagement ring, but Karli and I will also have huge fun hunting in the lovely Cairns shops for our dresses. She's thrilled to be my bridesmaid.

So that's my news.

I'm pleased that you're going up to Scotland to visit your father, and that you're going to invite him to our wedding. I'm looking forward to meeting him.

Good luck with finishing your book. I have my fingers crossed for you, but, honest to God, I'm your target audience and I think it's absolutely brilliant. Even I could end up wealthy if I followed your advice.

I'm sure every publisher who sees your manuscript will want to buy it. There'll be a bidding war, and very soon you'll be a famous author and the backs of your books will announce that you divide your time between London and a tropical island.

Your readers will think that sounds wonderfully romantic, and they'll be right. I'm sure they'll also think that your wife is the luckiest woman in the world—and they'll be right about that, too.

All my love, my kind, brilliant, sexy Englishman.

Until tomorrow, and all our tomorrows…

Molly xxxxxxxxx